MICHAEL WARD'S
SHORT STORIES

DORRANCE
PUBLISHING CO
EST. 1920
PITTSBURGH, PENNSYLVANIA 15238

Dorrance Publishing Co
585 Alpha Drive
Pittsburgh, PA 15238
Visit our website at *www.dorrancebookstore.com*

ISBN: 978-1-6386-7066-7
eISBN: 978-1-6386-7886-1

DEDICATION

I would like to dedicate this book to my best friend, my wife, Diane.
To who I admire and love so very much. To who I love to travel
with and all that we do together makes my life complete.
To all my children and grandchildren that I enjoy being with.

MISCALCULATED

As I sit at my desk searching information about our cruise for my wife, Alex, which is short for Alexandra, and myself, as the phone keeps ringing off the wall. I just gave up looking as I closed the website. I had so many orders to be filled and taking my time to research the cruise line was making me further behind. I only have 3 weeks before our vacation. We have not been away for the last 2 years since our work has grown into what it is today. My wife and I own a medical equipment company that we make in Japan, have blueprints that I have patented, and we make everything there and then they are shipped to us in Oregon, where we unload, then ship them all over America and some in Canada. I also go into everywhere that has medical equipment and we inspect them, and if they are in need of repairing we will do that but if they are outdated then we can upgrade the equipment, and also we have a maintenance agreement which we do an inspection once a year to ensure everything is working properly. We can also do quarterly inspections on medical equipment such as any life-supporting, monitoring and respiratory equipment to ensure everything is up to standards and repair or replace as needed. When I go into big companies and show them my proposal and I can do all inspections and repair and then every 4-5 years depending on the usage, I can bring the equipment in for a complete inspection and put a loaner in its place without their company having to do anything. With no down time or worrying about, it is a timesaver and they are all for it. With so many changes in the medical profession so many places are updating their equipment, and they are using someone who can do what I have and they are loving it.

We started the business with just the two of us, then we hired Gary, who is really a smart man and he fit right in with us. He just got back from a training seminar on shipping and receiving, I just put him in charge with handling this so that will give me some relief and not work so much in that department. I need to spend more time with my clients and try and get new ones. We developed a foam packaging system in which in Japan, once the equipment is ready for shipment all they do is place a plastic bag around it and place it in a box, then fill it with spray foam. It is quick and I never received a piece that was damaged due to shipping. Once here Alex records the numbers on the machine and it goes into our system, then we can keep a full history of that piece.

The shipyard is only 2 miles from our supply house and we have purchased 6 containers in which we use to ship products from Japan. Our company name is Henry-McGee, which is named after Alex and my family name, we just put them together. So we have our name on all 6 containers. We usually get 2 shipments every 4 weeks unless we are doing a new hospital or a large refurbishing at one time, then we will have an extra container come in. This being Friday, Gary will be back to work on Monday, then we can go over our orders and he can take it from there.

Alex stopped by to see if I needed anything, she was going to the mall to buy some shoes to go with her outfit she bought for our trip. She is more excited than I am. I told her we were going to Japan to check on the plant there and we were going to take a 5-day cruise while we were there. And we were only taking 2 days of clothing because we are going to buy all our clothes there, where the prices are much cheaper. She was thrilled with that but what I was really doing is booking us a flight to Hawaii, then go on a 7-day cruise around the islands. Alex has always dreamed of going to Hawaii and going on a cruise was her dream also, she will be so surprised. As I was researching for the trip someone gave me a name, John Wiley, he owns a large hospital there. During my studying him I learned he also owns a large clothing store, and some kind of security company. John is not a native Hawaiian but has been there for a long time.

I spoke with Mr. Wiley a few times and seems he is very interested in changing his medical equipment to my business, so I told him of my plans and we agreed to meet for dinner once we arrive to discuss a changeover. John would have someone pick us up at the airport and take us to the hotel, then later we would have dinner. I know this is supposed to be a vacation but since we will be there being face to face with a client is always better. Besides, he said he could take us to his clothing store and we could get name-brand clothes at wholesale prices. This was going to be a great trip.

When I got home Alex was making a Japanese meal, she said she wanted to get ready and she was also studying on how to speak Japanese so she could communicate with the workers in the plant there. She already had her 2 days of clothing set out ready to pack, she could not wait.

The following week with Gary was very busy and he knew we were going to Hawaii, he was the only one I told and he was ready to handle me being gone. I learned more about John Wiley, I thought the more knew the more likely he would turn his medical equipment to me. Seemes as if John came from money, his father made his money in the shipping business and John came into his money and he bought a large hospital, then a clothing mall, a security company, then a semi-pro baseball team. Everything he owned had nothing to do with the other businesses, which was odd but whatever works for him. His wife was from Hawaii and her family. I was hoping that I had enough information to impress John and gain his trust in my business.

I had 2 other hospitals I was working on and one was the owner of 5 hospitals in Washington and 1 in Montana, that was the one I was playing golf with this Saturday morning, so this week was busy. When the week was ending I was exhausted, having our trip all lined up and put up a false trip to Alex was getting difficult. I listen to her Japanese at night, I was really impressed. As Saturday morning arrived I had breakfast with Alex, then I had to go get some papers at the office, our tee time was at 1:12 so I had plenty of time. I arrived at the clubhouse a little early, didn't want to be late. I invited Mike Goodman, owner of the company, his son Samual, who was in line to take over the company, and Mike's son-in-law, James Snyder, all to play because I knew Mike was a family man and being all together wouldn't hurt.

Upon their arrival I had us all signed in and ready to play, the weather was beautiful, just a little cool breeze, a perfect day to play golf. Mike and I rode together while Samual and James rode in the other cart. They were all good players and they play a lot, so I had to really play good if I wanted to keep up with them. After we played 7 holes I stopped the beverage cart girl and I bought a round of beer, I was 2 strokes behind Mike and 4 behind James, Samual was having a hard day and was 2 behind me. After a great day of golf and discussing the equipment of my business and his hospitals, we ended up at the clubhouse for a drink. James bought the drinks because his score was a 76, one of his best, he said. Mike and I tied with an 81 and Samual with an 89. They had to leave because they had a 2-hour drive. As we walked to the car, I asked Mike if there was anything he needed me to do for him, he said to call his office Monday morning and he would get me the contact person to start with the changeout. He said he has been with the 2 medical equipment companies and he had never seen either one. I like being personal and I want my company to work with the same type of people. I told him thanks and we would do a great job and be safe going home. When I got home I called Gary and told him to get ready next week for getting a list of equipment for 6 hospitals, Alex was so pleased and told me to take a shower and she would have dinner ready, then I could relax.

The next day after church, we went over to our friends Johnny and Pat's house for lunch and watched football. Johnny and I grilled hamburgers outside while Alex and Pat made potatoes and baked beans, Pat also made some fried pies that we loved. As we spent some time talking about our trip to Japan, Alex spoke some Japanese and was so excited to tell all she had learned. It was hard for me to not talk about Hawaii but I kept my secret, even from my best friend. After we ate it was time for football, Seahawks against the Cowboys in Seattle. We watched football and talked about our work and how we were doing while Alex and Pat went into the kitchen and talked. The game was close throughout the entire game, it even went into overtime with the Cowboys winning with a field goal. On our way home Alex leaned against me and told me how happy she was and all that we have done. A beautiful ending to a beautiful weekend.

The next week flew by with us getting a contract signed with Mike, we were going to start changing out his hospital equipment each department at a time until one hospital was complete, then on to the next hospital until all were complete, starting the first of next year, so we had to get an inventory of what we were going to need so we could place our order in and be ready. Gary and I had 2 guys that did our onsite inventory research and they went all over to see what we needed to repair and replace. Hopefully by the end of December our warehouse should be fully stocked and ready to go. I had Gary check our orders in and record all the numbers on each piece of equipment, which that is what Alex did but with us being gone Gary was doing it. Making sure everything was in order, I left to go home and finish packing for our trip the next morning, Gary said have a good trip and he had everything in control.

As Friday morning arrived we were both up before the alarm went off, we drank some coffee and loaded everything in the car, we carried 2 suitcases each but hardly had anything in them because we were bringing back all the clothes we were to buy in Hawaii, well, Alex thought Japan. We had about an hour drive to the airport, I called the airport and told them of me surprising my wife and did not want to know where we were going until we boarded the plan, the airline was so nice and thought that was so romantic. They gave me a password and told me to give it to the person working the counter and it would tell them to keep it quiet. It worked, the lady at the counter checked us in and never mention our flight information. I kept Alex busy asking her certain words in Japanese, so she was so distracted that she never noticed our tickets, which I kept trying to hind the word Hawaii. After we went through the metal detector we went to sit at our gate, I kept her back to the gate and flight, as we sat down I took out a book about Hawaii and never said anything, just looking at the pages when the announcement saying, "Flight 3390 to Hawaii will be boarding in 20 minutes."

Alex looked confused and said, "I thought we had a direct flight."

"We do," I said, "but we are going to Hawaii for 2 days, then a 7-day cruise around the islands, not Japan."

"What?" she busted out in tears. "How did you do this?"

"We are not working except tonight we have dinner with a hopefully future client, and he also owns a clothing mall where in the morning we will be going to pick out our clothes for the cruise. Then just us."

She hugged me so tight, wiping tears away from her face, kissing me and holding me so tight. I felt so proud, giving my wife her vacation of her dreams and surprising her all this time. As we boarded the plane I told her in more detail of our plans for the next 10 days.

As we landed in Hawaii, we picked up our bags and looked for a man with a sign saying "McGee," he was our limo driver. As we walked to the limo he put our luggage in the trunk and we got in the back seat. On our drive we asked how far to the hotel but the driver said nothing, as we traveled it seemed as if we were going away from the city and 20 minutes later the driver pulled over. There were 4 men standing beside a van and one man opened the door and told us to get into the van, this seemed strange but we did and the limo driver took off with our luggage. I yelled to stop him and one man told me to be quiet and sit down as he pulled out a gun.

"What's going on, this is a mistake."

He said, "Are you McGee?"

"Yes," I said.

"Then this is no mistake," another man said.

When I asked questions they seemed to get angry and for me to be quiet if I knew what was good.

We arrived at a cabin, where they told us to get out and walk to the cabin, it was very small and looked if it was about to fall down. We went inside and two men went inside with us as the other two stayed outside. A door open from another room and a tall man came into the room where we were at and said, "Mr. and Mrs. McGee, sorry for they delay. I am John, we will be flying to another location, we are waiting for our sea plane to get here. Here is some water, you must be thirsty, please drink as we wait."

I said, "Where are we and who are you?"

"All you need to know is my name is John. Do what I tell you and no one will get hurt. There is a door to the toilet, as you can see no windows so there is no way to escape, just relax and wait."

We sat confused and scared, after about 2 hours we heard a plane and John went outside, then in a few minutes he returned and told us to get up and come with him. We walked down a walk, then onto a dock where the plane was waiting. One man open the door and shoved us in, the pilot was in there keeping the plane running while John got in behind us.

The pilot said, "Ready?" and John replied, "Yes."

As were got into the air we headed west into the sun, it was hard to see anything. It wasn't too far until I saw land and the plane circled the island, then headed down and then was flying just over the water. The pilot skidded on top of the water as we headed on to a cove, where there was a dock, and he rested the plane just a few feet from the dock as two men pulled up beside the dock and tied the plane up.

The door opened and John jumped out. "Let's go," he said, and we stepped on to the dock where a jeep was waiting with a large man driving.

We were told to get in the back as John sat in the front, the driver told us, "Buckle up, it is going to be a bumpy ride."

"Where is Mr. Wiley?" I asked.

"Quiet," he said.

As we traveled up the mountain it was very bumpy but we held on and were scared as to what was going to happen to us.

After about 15-20 minutes of being bounced around, we came to a stop at a parking area.

"Get out," John said, "and follow me up these steps to a house."

After a long way up to the house we stood on a deck, then a glass door opened and a man came out.

"Welcome to my house, Mr. and Mrs. McGee, I am Mr. Wiley, come in. Sorry for all the confusion but I have to be careful, some people don't like me and I don't want them to know where I live."

"Who can blame them, look at the way you treat people, we were scared to death," I said.

As John laughed he ordered a young girl to bring us dinner. "Come sit at my table, we can eat and then I will tell you my plan."

I told him, "My wife and I will not be treated this way, and we do not want to do business with someone like you."

"I admire that from a man, that is why I chose you. I needed someone I could trust and be a cover for me. I own a lot of businesses and many people respect me, I own companies and everyone thinks I am rich because of the companies I own but I do make good money, but I want power. That is how I made it possible for you to find me. I own the shipping company that transports the Henry-McGee containers and I have studied you for the 2 years. I know more about you and your company than Gary does."

Alex asked, "How do you know Gary?"

"His dad worked for me, that is how I hooked him up with you but you never knew it, neither did Gary, I just made contacts so you two could meet and knew he would fit in with you."

I said, "Gary never talked much about his dad, just that he had a heart attack on a ship."

"Well, he did die on a ship but it wasn't a heart attack, he was shot. You see, Gary's dad overheard me telling another employee something that wasn't to be shared with anyone else, and when he was about to talk I shot him. My people don't talk and if they do, well, bad things happen. You see, I want power and you are going to help me get it, your medical equipment will be a way to have power over America."

"My equipment saves lives, how will that get you power?"

John said, "Your blueprints will be altered, so let's say a heart monitor will display a heartrate 195 over 125 when actually it is 135 over 70, so the doctors will give medicine to lower the heartrate when it will be so low that the patient will go into a coma or die. Blood pressure with wrong readings. Defibrillators with a much higher charge than what is being called for. No one will ever know what is going on. I am in the process of having two of the largest medical equipment in America not only altering their new equipment but when they are in the inspection period of equipment that is being used they will not meet code and hospitals will have to change them out, and before long the majority of hospitals will have deadly equipment that read perfectly good and people will be dying and I will get my revenge."

"Mr. Wiley, why would I do that?"

"Because you love your wife and friends, if you don't then they will all suffer and wish they were dead," he said.

"We can't do that."

Mr. Wiley said, "Take them and lock them up."

The two men led us down the hallway into this room, opened the door and pushed us inside, then locked the door behind us. It was pitch black in the room so we held each other. We were worn out so we lay down and cried all night until we fell asleep.

We smelled coffee, then the door opened and a man took us into another room, where our luggage was sitting. The man told us to take a shower, then change clothes and hurry, Mr. Wiley would be waiting.

After we showered and got ready the door opened and a man told us to follow him. We entered a room filled with Japanese decorations, there sitting at a table was John Wiley drinking coffee.

"Sit," he said. "Have some breakfast and the best coffee you have ever tasted."

The table was set with all kinds of fruits with eggs, bacon, Spam, toast and jellies. We just sat there not putting anything in our plates, while John filled his plate he yelled for us to eat.

'You will learn that when I command you to do something you will do it."

"We are not hungry."

John told the man standing behind us to cut off my wife's left index finger.

"No!" I yelled as the man grabbed my wife's hand. I said, "Alright, we will eat."

John said, "First lesson, do as I say and don't ask questions."

Even though we were sick to our stomachs from being threatened, we still ate. The coffee was good and the fresh juices along with the rest was really good.

John said, "What I am about to tell you is something I haven't told many people, but I think you two need to know so you know why I am doing this. My mother is from Japan, she is a long line of Japanese descendants and I never knew my father, some U.S. Army guy who raped my mother and killed her parents and her grandmother. I am the result of my mother being raped. All my mother knew that he was in the Wiley division. After the war anyone with an American last name was given special privileges. So my mother gave me an American name, John Wiley, you met my son John Jr. already. So my plan is to get revenge and this may take a few years, but at least my son will have the power our family deserves. My mother did marry James, who owned the shipping company, that is how I got involved in the business. After his death he left the company to me, and for years I've been trying to find a way to get back to those who destroyed my family. After a lot of deaths America will discover that the companies they are buying from are sending malfunctioned equipment and a company in Japan can replace the deadly killing equipment they are using, then buy from Japan, giving back money they were robbed of."

Alex yelled, "You are sick, what is wrong with you?"

"Just getting back what was taken from my family." John told the man behind us to take Mrs. MeGee and lock her up. "Now, Mr. McGee, shall we go to the loading dock and begin our work?"

"No," I said, "I will not."

John told the man who had hold of my wife to remove all her clothing and have the other two men to come and visit her.

"Stop. I will do it, just don't hurt my wife."

"Alright, wasn't that easy? As long as you show false readings, then your wife will not be harmed."

John told the men in the warehouse to work me for 6 hours, then for them to let me eat for 30 minutes, then work 6 more hours and eat again, then work 6 hours, then let me sleep for 5 hours, then start over. After the workers had learned to follow instructions on altering the equipment, then he told me that I would be the inspector and to ensure everything went as plan.

"Your wife will be putting new I.D. numbers on each piece of equipment, that way we will know which has been recalibrated and is ready for delivery. I have called Gary and told him there was a delay in shipping and the containers would be 3 weeks late coming in," John said.

Gary was told that the shipping company had problems with the ship and was in repair but everything would be back to normal, and they have spoken to Mr. McGee and explained it to him and he knew all about it.

Greg called the warehouse in Japan and they did not know anything about the shipment being late and had not heard from the McGees. Gary knew he was in Hawaii on vacation and thought if there was a problem then he would call.

After two weeks we did the same thing day after day, and all the workers were now doing all the calibrating and I just inspected each piece, then Alex would be in the other warehouse recording new numbers on all equipment before being shipped. Finally Mr. Wiley brought Alex and I together and said he was giving us 10 hours alone, and we were escorted to another room where there was a bed, bathroom, and kitchen, where they had prepared food for us. He told us that we did everything he asked us to do and this was his way of saying thank-you. After we hugged and kissed we just held each other and were so thankful nothing bad had happened to either of us. We ate and freshened up, then we lay in bed talking about the last few days of being put through this nightmare. I told Alex that it was hard doing this, but I couldn't put her in harm even though what he was doing was wrong. She told me that when she put new numbers on the equipment that she put "GB" before the numbers.

"Gary knows we don't put letters on the ID numbers and hopefully he will realize that his initials are put before the numbers and something is going on. The first 2 containers should be arriving tomorrow, and let's pray that Gary doesn't ship them out after he discovers the wrong numbers on them."

"Listen to me, Alex, we have to try and escape, I've been watching and after they complete a shipment and they secure it no one is at the entrance because the guard has gone to get ready for the truck to come and pick up the container. After they take off with it, then they bring a new one but it takes 30-40 minutes. During that time no one is there, that is when we can leave. So Sunday, after you finish installing the last tag, wait 2 hours, then everything should be sealed and ready to be shipped. I have not been putting plastic around the equipment, just boxing them up and spraying foam around them. Gary will know that they don't ship that way in Japan and this isn't right. After you see the container loaded go tell John that you are having stomach cramps and you need to go lay down. Then I will go get supplies after the container is locked. The guard should be gone, so I will sneak out behind the container and go down under the dock and we will meet there."

Alex hugged me and said she didn't know if she could wait 2 more days.

As we lay there the door was unlocked and John Jr. yelled and said for us to get moving, our time together was over, and as we walked out he pushed Alex against the wall and looked at me and said, "Go ahead, do something," but we kept quiet and walked toward the warehouse.

We continued working, making sure our escape plan would work and keeping time on the guards as they worked and did the same routine every day.

As Sunday arrived I kept my supplies low so that after the last container door was shut and locked I could go restock my supplies and no one would suspect anything. The last piece was boxed and spray foamed, then loaded so everything was in place. I told the guard that I needed supplies and he let me through. The entrance doors opened, waiting for the crane to load the container on the truck. The guard was busy getting the delivery ready to be loaded. I walked past the supply room and kept close to the wall, and on the other side I saw Alex crawling under the crane heading to the dock. I ran past the truck and under the dock, where Alex was waiting.

"We made it," Alex said.

"Yeah, but we have to hurry because after they load the container a new one will be waiting to be unloaded, then they will close the doors. It won't take long for them to miss me and then they will look for you. We have 4-5 hours before it gets dark, so we need to get a head start. We need to split, you go west and I will go south. Go straight toward the sunset and wait for me."

"How will you find me?"

"Just listen for me, they will be on 4-wheelers and you can hear them for a long way, I will be walking and when you hear me call my name. We should alright, they will be looking at the beach thinking we will be heading to find a boat. Not ever looking in the mountains. Be careful and I love you."

"I love you too."

As Alex took off running west, I went south trying to make tracks for a while before heading west. I came to a stream so I went in and out going all different directions, trying to confuse them before I climbed a tree and jumped down and headed west. I ran west for a while, then turned north, trying to find where Alex went through, I saw where she walked and followed. After an hour or so I heard Alex, she was hiding under a bush.

After they unloaded the new container the doors were closed, the guard was checking things out and didn't see anyone in my area, he just figured it was break time. After the container doors were unlocked and opened, John Jr. came to see if everything was alright. He asked the guard where McGee was.

"The last time I saw him he was going to get supplies."

"When was that?" he asked.

"Just after we finished locking the doors on the container that left."

"Call my dad down here now."

As John and John Jr. gathered all the workers together, they asked if anyone knew where McGee was and no one said a word.

"Go check on Mrs. McGee and see if she is there and bring her to me down here."

As John Jr. went to check John called the transport truck at the loading dock and had them to open the container and see if they were inside. John Jr. ran down, saying that she was gone also. John ordered the guards to put all the workers in the supply room and lock the door and don't let anyone out until someone talks.

Alex had a bag with her with 2 bottles of water, some nuts and some bread.

I said, "Let's keep going to the other side of the mountain, then we will head down toward the water, hopefully far enough away that they will not look for us there. We have a bright moon so we can walk farther."

"But I am getting hungry," Alex said.

"Let's go a little more, than we can rest and eat."

Along the way we found bananas, mangos and almonds. So we stopped and ate, then we rested under some brush. After a short rest we awoke and I told Alex to bury the peelings so no one would discover them. As we headed down the mountain we came across a pineapple field, so we picked 4 pineapples and ate one of them as we walked, juicy and sweet, never had anything so good.

Mr. Wiley and his crew searched all along the beach, along the road to and from the warehouse until it was too dark. He said, "We will meet at the warehouse at 8:00 in the morning." He then went to the supply room and asked again if anyone knew where the McGees went. No one knew anything of their escape. "So if you are going to keep quiet then you will work double shifts, get that container unloaded and start to work."

The next morning the search party started at the warehouse and there were 4 men in 3 different parties and they all went in different directions. Mr. Wiley said the only way off the island was by boat so they must be around the beach. The first group headed south, the second group headed east and the third went west.

"We have to find them and if they resist them shoot them, but they cannot leave the island."

As the groups searched, the third party found a trail and followed it until they came to the stream. They looked everywhere and could not figure where the tracks were going. Finally they gave up and kept looking west.

As the shipment finally arrived in Oregan, Gary unloaded the container and noticed that the equipment was not bagged before the spray foam, so he called the warehouse in Japan and wanted to know what was going on. They swore that every piece was bagged before being foamed. Gary didn't know what to think, something was not right. Still no word from anyone. So Gary decided to call Mr. Wiley and ask if he heard from them and please have them call as soon as they could. Mr. Wiley was not in his office, but the lady that answered the phone said she had not heard from them but would ask and see if anyone else had any contacts and she would let him know.

We walked for 3-4 hours and Alex said she needed to take a break.
"Alright, but only long enough to eat some fruit and drink plenty of water."
One good thing about being in Hawaii is water is everywhere and fruit is plentiful, so being thirsty or hungry was not an issue.
"Let's walk down, we shouldn't be that far from the water."
As we walked we heard 4-wheelers so we headed back up the mountain. They were searching all around the island, covering the entire beach, so we had to head up away from them. The noise faded away as we continued to walk.
"What if they keep going up, what then?"
"Well, we will."
Just then we heard more noise towards the west.
"Let's head east, they are getting too close."
We took short breaks, long enough to get a good drink, and we would fill our bottles up every chance we got. With no noise in the last few hours I figured we were not in danger. When over the hill was John's house, we walked all the way back.
"Listen," I said, "we can sleep here, they will never look for us here."
"Okay, but let's get a little closer, I know there is a storage shed behind his house, maybe we can sleep in there upon the rafters. I've seen it and no one ever goes in there."

I told Alex, "The only way out is to hop a ride with the ship that transports the containers. And the next container will be ready Wednesday, so we need to have a plan ready. So until then we need to keep quiet and not get caught."

As Gary continued to search he decided to call the airlines, he found the flight number that we left out on and asked if the McGees were on Flight 3390 to Hawaii 3 weeks ago. The airlines could not give him any names due to security reasons but they could see if the return flight was complete, and when you make a flight to and from that is called a complete flight and they could answer that. After finding Flight 3390 there were 2 incomplete passengers but that was all they could tell him.

The search teams did not find any more trails or footprints, they made a complete search around the beach and found nothing.
"Let's call it a night, it's dark and we cannot search at night, besides the men are tired."
John told them to get a good rest and tomorrow they would see 2 groups up the mountain and keep 1 on the beach.

As Alex and I climbed up the attic of the shed we found a blanket, which we slept on, and it felt wonderful. After a good night's sleep we were awakened by the smell of coffee brewing. We heard the men talking and making plans on where they were going. This was Tuesday so we must be ready for tomorrow's shipment and our escape.

Gary was at the warehouse when he noticed not only was the equipment packed different but he noticed that the equipment ID numbers all started with the letters GB and we never used letters, only numbers. So Gary called Japan and asked about the tags, and they said that they were tagged with numbers, only just as they always did. So Gary put a hold on all equipment, those in Japan and those in his warehouse until he could find out what was going on. So he called the airlines to get a flight to Hawaii and there was one that left at 8:25 P.M. and arrived in Japan at 11:54 P.M. with the time difference. So Gary booked it and tried to call Mr. Wiley once more. When his office answered they said they just talked to John and he said that the McGees never showed up and he had not heard from them and he did not want to do business with someone like that.

It was now Wednesday and the freight liner would be leaving with 2 containers. We carefully climbed down the ladder from the attic and walked down to the dock, staying 40-50 feet away from the open. There was only one group that went down to the beach and no one else was around, they were getting ready to load the last container. As we approached the loading area we heard the guard tell the driver of the truck to come in and have a cup of coffee, that they were behind and it would be at least an hour before they were ready. We crawled up to a catwalk, where security normally walks at night but not during the day.

"Okay, Alex, we are going to crawl to the edge, then jump onto the container and the operator that loads us up will never see us."

"Oh, let's just jump in the truck and drive off."

"Alex, they would catch us, remember, the road is very bumpy and we couldn't drive very fast. This is the only way, we have to go now because we don't know how long the driver will be before he comes back."

When Gary landed in Hawaii he took a taxi to a hotel and rested before he was up when the clothing stores opened. At 9:15 he took another taxi to the mall, he wanted to be there when they opened at 10:00. It wasn't a long ride and Gary was there waiting, then they opened the doors and he asked where the manager's office was. Once inside the office he explained the problem and needed to find John Wiley. No one there could help him, the manager said, "He hardly ever comes in and when he does we don't talk to him."

"What a hard man to find, he doesn't come here and he is never at his office, where could he be?"

So he went to the hospital and talked to the administrator and he was of no help either.

John called the search parties and asked if they found any clues but no luck. He ordered the 2 groups that went east and west to continue up to the top of the mountain and the one on the beach to keep a lookout for any fishing boats and look for footprints in the sand.

Alex and I were now hugging the top of the container, just as the crane lifted us up onto the truck the driver took off the dock. I told Alex to hang on, it would be rough and hopefully the sun would not heat the metal too hot because it was 20-30 minutes to the dock. After a wild ride we came to the loading dock, where the ship was waiting. The captain was on deck because they were late and he wanted to get going. As the truck backed up to a conveyer they loaded us onto the ship. While the truck picked up another container to take to the warehouse all the deck hands scattered like ants, the captain yelled orders and they jumped.

I said, "Let's wait until they take off and go inside for lunch, then we will climb down and hide out in the lifeboats."

As the captain went inside, everyone seemed to calm down and most everyone went inside also.

"Now's our chance, follow me, Alex, and we should be safe but we have to be very quiet."

When we stepped onto the deck we ran to a lifeboat and crawled under the tarp and hid inside. We found a box that said "Emergency food supply." We opened it up and found water, we ate dried beef and some canned green beans and canned peaches. It was just what we needed, then we heard the captain walk by talking to the crew, saying secure the cargo and prepare to shove oft.

"Captain," we heard someone say.

"Yes, what is it?"

"We just received word from Mr. Wiley that we are not to leave the dock until every inch of this ship is checked."

"Well, it's his money and we will do whatever he says."

As Gary searched, trying to find out what happened to us, he went to the shipyard and talked to the controller. He said he was looking for a carrier coming from Japan going to Oregon.

"Well, if a ship is going to Oregon from Japan, they don't stop here. They go straight from dock to dock, unless they are using a private carrier and they stop. There are many shipyards on these islands, it would hard to find what you are looking for. My suggestion is to rent a float plane and try spotting it from the air, there are many around here and they would be glad to fly you."

Gary told him thanks and off he was to find a plane.

As John ordered his men to head to the dock and check the ship, Alex and I climbed out of the lifeboat on the outside, where no one was, and we walked to the end of the ship and we climbed under the walkway and down to the beach, where we hid behind a fuel truck, then we ran as fast as we could to the trees. Moments later there came 5 trucks with men who were the ones that were checking the ship, trying to find us. We felt pretty safe because everyone was concerned about the ship, so we headed to the other side of the island just far enough from the water not to be seen but close enough so we could hear a fishing boat.

When Gary hooked up with a pilot and told him of his story, the pilot said he was never a fan of the Wileys and he would be glad to help. The plane was only a few miles away. Derek, the pilot, said that they could grab a bagged lunch at the dock since it was after lunch now, He was getting hungry. Spam sandwich with chips and a bag of cut-up fruit, along with a soft drink. They were ready and as they started, then in no time they were in the air. So smooth, they flew around some big island, then headed north to some smaller islands, every shipyard they came in close to look but not the one they were looking for. After a couple of hours they headed east to another island, they flew around and they spotted a carrier with containers and as they flew closer he thought he saw it.

"Can we come closer?" Gary asked.

"Sure," Derek said.

As they took a wide turn he saw it: "Henry McGee" printed on the side. There it was, but what they also saw was a truck with guns mounted in it.

Derek said, "This can't be good, that is illegal and that is nothing but danger."

I was looking for some water when Alex yelled, "A plane, there is a plane!"

"Don't let them see you, it might be the Wileys searching for us."

As the plane circled we noticed on the side of the plane saying: "Derek's sightseeing company."

"It can't be them, they would have their own plane."

As Alex came out of the woods waving her hands, the plane flew low, then circled back.

During the ship search, John Jr. saw the float plane and took 3 men with him to where the plane circled.

As Alex and I stood in the clearing of the beach, the plane came just above our head.

Gary said, "It's them, let's land this thing and pick them up."
Derek headed to the west, then back to the beach, so the wind was just right, he flew in low landing on the water, then toward us. When the plane was on shore the door of the plane opened and Gary got out.

We ran toward him and asked, "How did you find us?"
He said, "Get in, we can talk later, this plane has to draw attention."
As we turned toward the water we took off, and I just knew John saw us and would be following us.
"Listen," Derek said, "I am taking you to my brother's house on another island, we can stay there until we can get a flight back to Oregon. My brother is gone for a couple of months and I look in on his house now and then. I can put my plane in a covered dock and we will be safe tonight."

John Jr. arrived as we were going out of sight, he called his father and told him we must have been on that plane. John called his connections and told them to be on a lookout for a float plane leaving his island and follow them. "Don't let them leave," he commanded.

We circled the small island and landed and coasted to this broken-down dock, then went through some low tree branches, then we entered a beautiful covered dock with a cute little house. We secured the plane, then went into the house, where we started talking about the last 3 weeks. After we told Gary of our experience and what we were made to do and John's plan to destroy America, he said he noticed the ID numbers having GB in front.
"I knew something was going on, but when the equipment came in unwrapped I stopped everything and started looking for you guys."
"Hey," Derek said, "how about some grilled porkchops and frozen corn, my brother always keeps his freezer stocked."

"Let me cook," said Alex, "it's been 3 weeks since I cooked anything."

No one argued and as she was cooking we talked about what we needed to do to have John arrested.

"We need to get a flight back home, I need to make sure our warehouse in Japan is not sending any more equipment out until we get this straight."

Gary said he already put a stop on all supplies being shipped out.

After our meal we showered, then to bed, tomorrow may be a long day.

John Wiley put 2 men at the airport looking for us and he had his helicopter flying around the islands. They had to fly from the airport and he told his men to stay there until they found us. He had 2 other men checking the cruise line dock and he thought they may have tried to catch a cruise.

When Gary knocked on our door the next morning, he said the 3 of us had a flight at 12:17 this afternoon. So Derek said he could take us to the police and have them handle this, we decided that would be the best thing to do.

"What if the Wileys have connections to the police?"

"Then we would be dead for sure."

Just then Gary's phone rang, it was John Wiley, Gary answered.

"Hello, this is Gary…yes, sir, they are back home, they arrived early this morning, I am to meet them for dinner tonight."

Gary said he hoped that he had a chance to talk to him and hoped they could have his hospital business but would get more information at their meeting and would get back to him, then he hung up.

"So he thinks you are back in Oregon, so he won't be checking the airport."

"Gary," I said, "how brilliant, you just opened the airport for us."

Derek said, "Let's go to his dock, then he can drive us to the airport."

When we got there we told Derek to come in and have lunch, we had time. He said he couldn't, he had a sunset tour this evening but for us to take care.

"How much do we owe you for dinner last night and taking us here?"

"Not a thing, just put the Wileys in jail, that is my fee."

We shook hands and parted ways. As we sat eating lunch still keeping an eye out, we discussed what our next step was.

John was trying to figure out on how to get to the McGees before they went to the police, so John and John Jr. took a private plane to Oregon to catch us before our meeting. He thought we had not gone to the police since we had a meeting with Gary this evening.

After we landed the 3 of us went straight to the police department, where we told the chief our story and thought Homeland Security, FBI, CIA and anyone else we needed to talk to should be contacted. We were escorted to this conference room where we waited, then the FBI came in and talked to us, then Homeland Security came in and we told them the same thing, they told us to wait and brought us some coffee. After a while they came in and told Gary that he was not needed anymore and to go to the warehouse in case he was needed, he agreed and left the room. When the FBI came back they told us to go with them. We went into a smaller room, where they told us to fill out some reports and don't leave out any details, they would come back later.

Mr. Taylor entered the room and said he was over Homeland Security and he would be the only one that would be talking to us from now on. He said, "I know this has been a long day but there is still a lot to do." Mr. Taylor said, "They know John Wiley is in Oregon and is looking for us, he said they have men watching the warehouse and that we will be in contact with him shortly. There is an agent with Gary as we speak and Gary is going to call Mr. Wiley so they can locate where his is, then he will be arrested."

"Great," Alex said.

"I need you 2 to be here when we bring them in."

"Why?" I asked. "You have our story, what else can we do?"

"Just be patient," Mr. Taylor said.

After Gary's phone call to John, the FBI was following him and when he turned toward the warehouse his car was stopped and 12 agents covered his car. They took the Wileys to the police station and took both of them into a room beside us, we could see and hear them but they could not us. They told John what he was accused of: kidnapping.

"What are you saying?" I yelled.

"Be quiet and listen. John told them that we were the ones who took over. That we hijacked the transporter ship and took it to a warehouse in Hawaii, where we recalibrated the equipment that they were transporting from Japan to Oregon. Then they shipped it to the warehouse here, that is why we came here, to stop the selling of malfunctioned equipment to healthcare and stop thousands of deaths. John was almost in tears talking about it. He really made a believable story and the FBI came and told us to come with them."

We entered where the Wileys were sitting, and then Mr. Taylor came over and handcuffed Alex then myself and said we were under arrest for tampering with medical equipment and attempted murder. We were escorted out and we kept saying it was them, not us.

After we left they put us in an unmarked car and drove us to a pizza parlor, where no one else was in there. They took us inside and removed the handcuffs and told us to sit and be quiet.

As the Wileys sat there looking at each other, they couldn't believe what has just happened. The FBI thanked them for stopping what could have been a disaster and asked if there was anything they needed for their time.

"Not a thing, just glad to be of help," John said.

When they got onto their private plane, they thought how they escaped prison but they just lost a lot of time and equipment. He told his son that they had to work on plan 2, now this was at a standstill for now. They took off for Hawaii, being free.

While we sat they brought us a pizza and a glass of wine and told us to enjoy.

"Listen, you have made a terrible mistake, we are not the ones who should be here. You let the Wileys go when they should be here."

He said nothing and left the room.

"Listen, Alex, I don't know what to do, we may go to jail."

The waiter came back and asked if we needed anything.

I said, "I want Mr. Taylor in here."

The waiter told us we would be here for a while, maybe all night, so drink and eat.

It seemed like hours when Mr. Taylor came and got us and took us back to the police station. Alex started crying and saying this was a mistake.

"Just calm down, you two, and follow me."

We went into this dark office, where three other men were sitting. One man turned and said they were sorry for the last few hours, but it had to look as though we were taken into custody and we could not talk to anyone.

I said, "We are confused."

"Look at the monitor, you see the Wileys? They just arrived in Hawaii, and we have a squad waiting for them, we are following them to their warehouse, where we will arrest them and bring them to Washington, D.C. We found out that John Wiley has a long list of illegal businesses, along with attempting murder, kidnapping, drug ring in Japan, and selling stolen goods, but this with the medical equipment will put him behind bars for life and we thank you for your help. And for all your help the transport ship which was seized and is in the process of being put in Henry McGee's company, so you now own a transporter so you can control your own shipping. We also know that we were to go on a cruise around Hawaii, so we are giving you a 10-day cruise anywhere, didn't know if Hawaii was still your dream vacation or not. Now go and get some rest, you two deserve it."

As they drove us to our house, Alex asked, "How did you know where we lived?"

"We're the FBI, we know everything."

MY LOST TREASURE

Growing up in a small fishing town, everyone worked with or had some kind of connection with fishing, I loved being around boats. My childhood was simple, I went to school and most evenings were spent around the boat docks. I would help fishermen as they got ready for the next morning outing, which came very early. They gave me money, sometimes fish for me to take home to my family. Some of the fishermen would take me out on the water when they were checking out things or trying something new. It was wonderful being out on the water, so peaceful and relaxing.

As I grew older, my boating experience grew and I could sail a boat like a pro, being only a teenager, my father was so proud of me. I loved the water and loved fishing, my father, who always worked for other people, did not have much time to enjoy his time off. This made me work harder and I set my goal to have my own business. Once I completed school and got some experience, I would own a business of my own.

With a degree in business, I worked in a construction company. I was in charge of ordering and selling material to contractors, which we were the only ones close to the busy construction sites. My love for the water was becoming less and less, I spent so much of my time working and trying to save up money so I could have my own business that my sailing was becoming less and less. As time allowed I would try and get information about different items I could sell and make a living, trying to find out what people would need that was not available.

I came up with the idea of a control system to which people could control their lighting either by a timer or by computer. I could install a system so the owner could turn on or off lights in their home or business, also control the temperature. After a couple of years and getting a loan, I started my own business. It grew so fast, I had so many contractors buying from me and I just started selling to the public. But my love for the water was still there.

After my father passed away from a massive heart attack, I knew he worked so hard and never enjoyed his life, so I decided to bring in a partner to help since this company was getting out of hand. I knew we would expand and I could not do it alone.

My girlfriend and I enjoy as much time as work will allow, which is not enough according to her. Every now and then I go sailing but my girlfriend thinks it is a waste of time, she hates the water. I know my personal life is hurting but the business is really busy. After my girlfriend left me I took a look at my life and I was following my father's footsteps, work, work, work. That was all he did so I could have a better life, and that is what I am doing also. I spent so much time at work that I might as well sell my house because I lived at the office. Derek, my partner, and I discussed about hiring someone that could help us so we could take time off, we thought if we trained someone to work full time we could take a few days off, taking turns, this way we would not kill ourselves and we could enjoy life. I was not going to end up like my father.

After a year of training Greg on doing what we were doing, Derek and I were able to take off a few days and everything was working great, so we decided to take off a week at a time, and we could be away and the company would not suffer.

My love for sailing when I was younger was still with me, and I would sail all day whenever I wanted. Derek took 2 weeks off, so his wife and young daughter took a long vacation. Once he returned it would be my turn. During my excitement of being off for two weeks I searched for a sailboat to rent for two weeks, after finding one they would not rent it until I took a 2-hour lesson with them so they knew I was able to sail. When our lesson was over I signed the papers and had it rented for 2 weeks starting the following Monday. With 4 days until taking off, I made a list of what I would need to take with me, I decided to sail east for a day, then turn around and come back the next day, then a couple of days later I would head north for 5 or 6 days. There were some islands I wanted to visit just a few miles away and I wanted to sail around them, then I would bring the boat back and maybe someday I would buy myself one and sail wherever I wanted.

The day before I was to leave I packed some fruit, some cheese and French bread, along with some ham and a bottle of wine. I packed 6 water bottles and some fruit bars that should keep me full until I got back. After a restless night being excited about my journey, my alarm went off and up I was. I made myself coffee and eggs and bacon with toast, this would stay with me until this evening, when I would be on the water. As I loaded up the ice chest I put the bottle of wine in the bottom and the ice on top of it and the rest on top of the ice. I decided to take a wine glass and a knife to cut the ham and cheese. I only took a pair of shorts in case I wanted to go swimming if I got too warm. This was all I would need except I took a rod and reel with a couple of lures just in case I might get the urge to catch a fish, I could not cook it but the ice would stay in the ice chest until I returned. When I arrived at the dock I parked my car in the parking lot and I walked to the boat, I had memories of my childhood, the fresh air early in the morning, the saltwater, there was nothing like it.

After loading the boat, the gas can was full so I put all 5 gallons in the tank, knowing I would not need much but one never knows. As I started the motor I untied the lines and off I went. As I got going the wind was perfect, so I killed the motor and lifted the sails and sailing I was. It did not take much wind to move the small boat, slight breeze, warm temperature in the 70s, what a day. As I traveled east my plan was to go as far as I could, then turn around in the morning and head back and dock around dark the next day. As I tied the wheel to stay on course I sat back and enjoyed. Every now and then I would see a larger boat passing by, but all I could hear was the waves. I enjoyed a juicy pear and a bottle of water as I sailed along, feeling as if I was the only one on the water. As time flew by I could tell it was going to be sunset shortly, so I opened the ice chest and cut the ham into bite-sized pieces and the cheese, along with grapes and strawberries. The French bread I sliced and opened the wine and poured me a glass. What a meal with the sun setting over the water, beautiful. I sat and took my time in eating and drinking the wine. I watched the sun disappear over the water as if it sank it the ocean. After a much refreshing meal I put the remaining food in the ice chest to save for tomorrow.

As I sat back and drank another glass of wine I felt so at peace, as the wind picked up I let down the sails because I did not want to travel too far or too far out, I just coasted along. I just lay there looking at the stars. I must have fallen asleep because when I awoke the boat was rocking and there were no stars in sight. I turned on the lantern as I saw the compass was pointing south. The boat was too hard to handle, I must be caught in a storm, where did it come from, and I was wondering what time it was. How long had I been asleep and how far south did I travel?

As I fought to keep the boat from flipping over, I could not see anything, it was dark, no moon, no stars, only clouds. What seemed like a couple of hours, I heard a loud crash and I was thrown into the floor. Water was gushing in the boat, I got up and thought I had to speed up to keep the water level above the hole in the boat. I started the motor and gave it full throttle, as I rushed through the waters I could make out a beach, the clouds were breaking so I could barely make out land, so I put it in full speed and right before I hit land I would cut the engine and glide upon the beach, and this would keep from harming the lower unit of the motor. I had it full throttle when I shut it off and lifted the motor and beached the boat upon the sandy beach. I took my light and saw the hole in the boat and knew I could do nothing until morning, so I climbed into the boat and would rest until daylight.

As I slept in the boat, the sun peeked over the boat and I awoke, not being clear of what happened. It took a minute, then I realized I was shipwrecked. Where am I and how do I get help? As I studied the damage I knew I could not use the boat. How long could I last on 4 bottles of water, some ham and cheese with bread and a handful of grapes? I must find some help, there must be someone close. I ate some ham and the grapes and took some water, and I was off to find some help. To the south was rough, there was no beach, only large rocks, and out in the waters they were sticking up above the waves, to the north was sandy beach so that was the directions I would go. Hopefully I would see a resort or house, anyone who could help me. I walked and walked and saw no one, I did notice palm trees and banana trees along the way but found nothing ripe. My feet were hurting so I sat upon a fallen palm tree and finished my water. I decided to go deeper into the trees and see if maybe someone may be further inland. Bananas trees everywhere but only green ones and I didn't feel like having stomach issues. The farther I walked the more concerned I got, what if there was no one else here on this island? How long could I survive? My worries were really taking a hold of my mind, I might not ever get rescued. Then I heard water running, it was a spring. I tasted the water and it was fresh, ice-cold water. I filled my bottle and marked the trail with stacked limbs so I could find my way back.

As I made my way back to the boat, I marked my trail and knew I had to go back to fill my empty water bottles tomorrow, but now I would eat what was left and rest. Tomorrow I would try and find some fruit and try to catch some fish, I might be here a while. It was a cool night and being exhausted I slept all night, I made a nice bed in the boat and knew tomorrow would be a tough day.

As the sun alarm clock peeked over the side of the boat I climbed out, took a dip and gathered the water bottles, and took off to refill them with the fresh spring water. During my return I did find a few bananas I picked and they should be ready to eat. I thought I would try and catch some fish so I would have something to eat. All I could catch was little bait fish, nothing big enough to eat but maybe I would use them for bait, and I hooked the small fish onto the line and threw it as far as I could. It seemed like an hour but I got a bite and I hooked a big fish, as I reeled it in I knew I had dinner. I cleaned the fish and put it in the ice chest so I could keep it until I could build a fire and cook it. I dug a hole and put the guts in it, hoping I might catch some crabs as they ate the fish guts. I made a firepit and stacked some leaves and tree limbs and made a fire with the lighter in the supply box. I put the fish on a stick and cooked the fish over the hot coals. With fish and bananas and cool water, I was stuffed. Before it got dark I took three sails and made a cover over the boat so I would have shelter in case of rain. I fell asleep inside the boat and slept all night.

When I awoke I noticed the fish guts had been all eaten, I knew crabs would be back if I caught more fish. I ate a banana and drank some water, took my daily dip in the ocean, and tried to catch more fish. I had good luck, I landed 3 nice fish and cleaned them and put them in saltwater I put in the chest. I put the guts in the hole and waited for some crabs. I stacked palm leaves around the back side so they would not see me. As I walked through the jungle I found some mangos and they were ripe, so juicy, as I ate one and brought back an armful. I noticed some crabs going into the hole to eat, so I ran and got the oar out of the boat and started hitting the crabs because I could not pick them up with their big claws. After me swinging away at the crabs I ended up with 4 large crabs.

I knew I could not catch fish every day and not knowing how long I was going to be stuck here. I figured the boat rental would not be aware of me being gone until my 2-week rental was up, then to begin a search for me might take a week or two so I'd better get prepared for a few days here. I thought smoking some fish and with fruit scattered around, I could try and go farther inland, I could travel a couple of days, then return. As I made a bag out of the sail I loaded up with my water bottles, which I would refill, and wrapped my smoked fish along with some cooked crabs and off I went. I went to my water station and filled the bottles, then inward I headed. It was warm with no breeze, I walked and walked until I had to sit and have a bite to eat, as I sat and enjoyed my crabs I picked two mangos to go along with my crabs and my cold water. Resting against a tree, I heard water, like rushing water. I gathered my stuff and headed towards the sound, it was not long until I reached a river and I walked along to where I found a deep body of water. I felt the water and it was cool, being hot and tired I decided I would take a dip and cool off. I stripped and jumped in, wow, it was cold, I did not expect it being that cold. Once I caught my breath, I soaked and relaxed. Then I noticed on the other side there was a waterfall and I swam over to it and it was a beautiful small waterfall. As I was watching the water flow I saw something behind the waterfall, it looked like a box, so I made my way through the fall and could not believe my eyes. It was a chest, three chests, very old, with locks on them. What could this be? I took a large rock and hit the top of the chest and it split open, the wood was rotten so it did not take much to open. As I removed the top wooden lid I found coins, this was a treasure chest, I found a treasure chest, what kind of coins had I found? I opened the other two and they were filled with the same coins. I have found a hidden treasure, I was rich. I just sat there looking at the coins, trying to figure out what they were and wondering how long they had been there. I took a handful and headed back to where my clothes were, there I dressed and headed back to the boat, about every 50 yards I stacked some logs to mark a trail so I could find my way back to my treasure, being so excited I forgot to pick some fruit coming back. I got back just before dark and I made a fire, hoping someone would see it. I sat and drank my water and ate the rest of my smoked fish. I needed to make a plan on how to get the coins back here. No, I couldn't have them with me when I got rescued, this was my treasure, my secret, no one would get this, it was all mine. All night I studied the coins, no date, no symbols I could recognize, must be Spanish coins.

I knew I had to keep my body going, so fish and fruit, that was all I had. I knew I had at least a week before anyone would miss me, so I had to keep going. I would get up in the mornings and go swimming, then gather some fruit and fill my water bottles, then fish and rest until night, then catch some crabs and smoke fish. I would think about getting my treasure all day and all night, making it hard to sleep. I was going to be rich and when I got married and had kids they would never have to want for anything. My life was going to change.

Fishing was getting harder to catch fish, I had to catch bait, then use the bait to catch bigger fish, not having any luck I had to wade out chest deep, then threw out as far as I could, this was where the fish were. As I waded out I threw my line out a long way, I backed up letting out line as I backed out of the water, I was about knee deep when a fish nearly took my rod out of my hands, I set the hook and out he went, taking my line with him, I would reel in, then he would take it back out, we did this for twenty to thirty minutes. I had no strength left, then my line had slack in it, he was swimming towards me so I reeled in and walked backwards, at the same time hoping not to lose him, then it happened, I stepped on something, some kind of fish, my whole body went numb, I dropped my rod, I could not move. I fell backwards and crawled to the shore. Blood was coloring the sand red and I was in such pain. I managed to crawl to the boat and climb in just as I passed out.

When I woke my foot was burning with fire, I found a bottle of water in the boat, as I took a drank I passed out again from the pain. That was all I remembered until I awoke in the hospital.

When I opened my eyes I knew nothing, a nurse told me I was going to be alright, they saved my foot.

"Where am I and what day is it?"

She said I had been in the hospital for six days.

"How did I get here?"

"A plane found you in your boat, you have a bad sunburn and your foot was badly cut and you had blood poisoning. Did not know if we could save your foot, but we did and you are getting much better. Here is some soup, try it."

"That was the best vegetable soup I have ever eaten, how much longer will I be here?"

"Well, the doctor said you need a few more days of therapy, then you should be able to leave."

I slept the rest of the day and the next morning after breakfast I had more exercise for my foot, then as I went back to my room Mr. Taylor from Taylor's Boat Rental came to visit me.

"How are you?" he asked.

"Lucky to be alive, they tell me."

"You sure are lucky, to survive that storm that came from nowhere."

"Hey, I am sorry about your boat."

"Don't worry, the insurance will take care of it. Your car is safe and you can get it whenever you get out."

"Thanks, Mr. Taylor, it should be a couple of more days."

During my time in the hospital, all I could think of was my treasure. The morning of my release I had Derek come get me and take me to get my car, on the way I asked Derek about the guy who found me.

"Who was the guy who found me? How can I get hold of him?"

Derek was silent, then he said the man who found me had a plane wreck and was killed. A day after he rescued me he was landing his plane and crashed it.

"How did he spot me, how did he land his plane on the island?"

"All I know is he found you, rescued you, then took you to the hospital."

"So no one knows where he found me?"

"No," Derek said. "The hospital said the morning he came to visit you, then a few hours later they brought him in but it was too late."

As we arrived at my car, I got out and told Derek I would be back at work day after tomorrow.

"That will be great."

"I need to do some things before I return to work."

When I got into my house and put everything up that I brought back from the hospital, there it was, my little box of coins. I placed them on the living room table and sat to relax my foot, which was aching a little. I called my brother, who lives in West Florida, which is about five hours away. We talk but rarely do we visit more than once a year. After our talk I went to get some hot tea and went to bed, I slept like a baby. Being in my own bed felt so good.

The next morning I went back to the hospital and asked if anyone knew the name of the guy who rescued me. A nurse told me he was a close friend and his name was Billy Berry, everyone called him B.B. and he was killed a few days ago. She started tearing up, so I just asked if he had any family and she said only a sister, whom she knew nothing about. I told her if she knew if B.B. would have told someone where I was at when he rescued me.

"Well, I do know he had 2 planes, one a 6-passenger and a float plane," which was the one he picked me up in. "He kept them at the small private airport, which is about five miles south of the hospital, right on the beach."

I hugged her and thanked her for her time and the information.

I drove to the airport, and as I got out of my car a security officer told me this was a private section of the airport and only members were allowed. I told him what I was looking for and he directed me to another part of the airport. I walked through a gate and into another sidewalk, which led me toward a glass door. Once inside I walked to the counter where a lady was sitting. As I told her my story and what I was looking for, she started crying.

"I'm so sorry," she said, "but he was such a good man, and what a waste it was that he was killed. He loved to fly and to help people. He flew at least twice a week and always flew when someone was lost or missing. I did know he had his own business and must have a lot of money."

I asked about records. "Does the airport keep records of planes that leave the airport."

"Not private planes, the only records that we keep here are the time of take-off and time of arrival but nothing else. There was someone who came and picked up his other plane yesterday, I cried as it left the airport. We will really miss him. Never knew of a nicer guy and a more giving man."

I thanked her and returned to my car, where I was stunned. Someone had to know where I was found.

On my way home, I stopped by the city library and checked out a couple of books on old coins. That night I read all I could about old Spanish coins, then I studied my coins but with no luck with the books I had I went to bed to catch some sleep, tomorrow was back to work.

Wherever I was, those coins were in my head. Every spare minute I had was dedicated to finding out what they were worth. As I managed my work along with my research on coins and also trying to figure out where it was that I was stranded, time flew by. My search went from days to months to years. During which I meet my wife, I was in an exhibit of old ships when we met. I was finding information on ships that came here from Spain, maybe I could find something about my coins. My wife, Laura, loved history and we made a perfect match. We did not date too long before I asked her to marry me. To my surprise we had a baby boy a year after we were married. We did everything together. My search for the island I was on and the coins I found was a hobby Laura and I did. She gave up after a couple of years but I kept looking.

One day I charted a float plane and I wanted to see how far one could fly without running out of fuel. We flew over some small islands but too small where I was at. It seemed that a float plane could travel about two hours before heading back, that would be four hours with a full tank of fuel. I know I sailed further than that, but B.B. picked me up in his float plane, just didn't make sense.

As time went by my son was growing up and I wanted to teach him to sail, this way we could spend some quality time together and I could teach him something that he could use for the rest of his life. John, my son, knew how much time my lost treasure took and how it controlled me. This was a way we could be together and he could control the boat. He was a master, in no time John could sail a boat by himself and knew the wind and how to use the sails. About once a month we went sailing and it was great, as John grew older our sailing was getting less and less. I was back into searching for my island, and it kind of turned into an addiction. I was spending very little time with the family and had my game room at my house turned into a search-and-rescue. I had maps scattered everywhere and books about old coins. Stories of buried treasure and lost treasures. Everywhere you looked was some kind of studies of the 1600s and 1700s.

When John graduated college, Laura and I bought him a sailboat, it needed work but was sturdy. He was so proud and he worked on it every weekend. Durning the end of the summer John told his mother and I that this coming Sunday he was taking us sailing in his boat. He was taking care of everything, all we needed to do was be ready at 9:00 in the morning. When Sunday was here John came to the house and picked us up. He had a lunch packed and was ready to take us on a day of sailing in his boat. As we walked up the dock to his boat I noticed a large cloth draped across the back side of his boat.

"Dad," John said, "do the honors and unveil the boat."

As I removed the cloth, tears came to my eyes. Across the back were the words "The Lost Treasure." I was so proud of him and at the same time so sad. I knew I spent too much time researching only to come up empty.

We loaded up and off we went, spending the whole day sailing and enjoying our time together. As the day came to an end, we docked the boat and headed home. I couldn't stop thinking of my sailing disaster and what it had done to me. I asked John to come inside and thanked him for a wonderful day at sea and told him how proud I was of him. We sat at the table and I told John that I wanted to make him a partner in the company. He had worked there through high school and college. With a degree in computers and his knowledge of the business, I could not hire anyone more qualified. Tears came to his and his mother's eyes and I said I was not going to work so much and needed for him to take over.

So the next few months John took over and I backed out so he could take control. This gave me more time to do more research. I meet an old school buddy and he told me of this guy who knew everything about old ships, I did not tell him about my searching for coins but he knew I liked old ships. I got his address and it was not but a ten-minute drive to his house. I called to set up a time that I could meet him and he agreed. As I drove up to his house I noticed a very pretty yard, flowers everywhere. I walked up to his front door and rang the doorbell, he opened the door and told me to come in. He was a much older man than I expected.

"Come into my study," which was like being in a museum.

On every wall were displays of ships. Books wall to wall, tables stacked with old artifacts.

"Wow," I said, "how long have you been collecting?"

"Over sixty-five years, this is my life."

"Well, can you tell me about these?" then for the very first time I exposed my coins.

He sat wide-eyed and took one and examined it with a magnifying glass and a bright light.

"1600s from Ireland. I never looked for Ireland coins, Spain, Mexico, England, but never Ireland. Where did you buy these and how many do you have?"

As we sat I told him of my disaster and the chest of coins I found, "only I am unable to return to get the rest. Lost on an island, I know not where."

"Well, then let's start looking and see if we can find some lost treasure and where they were heading to and what happened to them. Come into my other study, here are some books, we can start looking at ships from Ireland in the 1600s and any stolen coins."

Every shelf was books about old coins, then above that was about ships that were wrecked and sunk.

"Let's start with ships that were stolen and then we can look for stolen money. Would you like a glass of wine? This will be time consuming, so might as well get comfortable."

We studied for hours and realized it was getting late.

"Let's call it a night," I said, "did not mean to take up so much of your time."

"I enjoyed it, I feel excited about doing research for a purpose again. Come back in the morning and we can start our search."

I said, "Mr. Henry, I've been searching for over 25 years."

He laughed and said, "Goodnight, see you in the morning."

"I'll be here around 9:00 A.M."

When I got home Laura had dinner ready, as we ate I told her of Mr. Henry's house and all he had in there, and how he was helping me look at Ireland. After we had dinner we watched a movie together, then went to bed, could not tell you anything about the movie, my thoughts were of stolen ships. I had a good night's sleep and was up early and ready to go to Mr. Henry's house.

When I drove up to his house he was outside watering his plants.

"Good morning," I said.

"Yes, it is. Come in, let's get started, I have a pot of coffee on the table whenever you want or need some. I found these books here, you start looking here and I will look at these."

After hours of reading I had to take a break.

"Care if I look around at your collection?"

"Go ahead," he said, "someone needs to enjoy them."

I had never seen so much information about ships, Mr. Henry's study was so amazing that one could not see all he had in a day. There were pieces everywhere stacked on top of each other, piled high, there was not an empty spot in the room.

After a few minutes of looking around, I got back to business. The book I picked up was about stolen ships in the 1600s. Within an hour I came across a ship that left Ireland on March 17th, 1657, it was to come to the free world but never arrived. The records they kept were very detailed and hopefully I could find some records on this ship. It was about 3:00 and I ordered a pizza so we could continue our research.

We went through so many records before coming across information about this ship that was stolen by pirates the day before it was to depart for the new world. We found out it had tobacco, potatoes, corn and cotton loaded, ready to be shipped off, when it was stolen. There was so much we were looking at that I did not realize it was already dark outside.

"It's late, I need to be going."

Mr. Henry said we needed to take the next day off and give our brains a rest.

"Alright," I said, "but the next day I may bring my son to help us, he would love to see your display."

After taking a break for a day, John came with me to Mr. Henry's house and when we walked in he had made us some fruit pies and coffee. As we enjoyed this treat John looked over all the ships on display.

"Can you tell me about some of these?"

"Sure thing. Over here is some pieces of a ship my grandfather was on, but it has 'Captain Cook' on it. That's my grandfather."

"But your name is Henry."

"Yes, Henry Cook. Everyone calls me Mr. Henry, but my last name is Cook. These pieces have been passed down to me, you see, I have saltwater in my blood. Enough about me, I have contacted a professor who studies old coins and he is letting us go to the university where he teaches and he wants to see what you have. It's only a thirty-minute drive and he said we could meet him at 10:30, so let's load up some information we have and head over there. Don't mind if I drive?" he said. "I need to get my car out more often."

We got in his 1965 Impala, he drove us to the university, which took about forty-five minutes, he was not a fast driver but we enjoyed our talk as we traveled. Once inside Professor Taylor met us and we entered his lab where he taught.

"Let me see what you have."

As I took out my box of coins and laid it on the desk, he removed one and just stared at it. Then he held it up to a light and used a powerful magnifying glass, writing down the symbols and words. He put it down and told us to get comfortable, it might take a while. He went to his computer and started his search, we compiled the things we found and had them all laid out in this long table. Professor Taylor came over and asked if we had any idea of what we had.

"No," I said, "only that they were Irish coins."

"Yes, uncirculated coins. In 1638, the Irish coins were changed to a new type of metal, which did not last long, the salty air rusted the new coins and in a few years they had to make new coins out of silver and gold. In 1655, the government was making the new money with a different value and it was to take effect January 1658. So in 1657 they were making the new coins and the government had to make the coins in the eastern part of Ireland and take them to the western part and have them stamped and dated, this was to keep control of theft. If the coins were ready to be used, then it would be hard to keep them from being stolen. This way they could make all the coins and store them until they were ready to be exchanged. During that time a group of English pirates raided the building the coins were stored in. They got caught and only a few got away. The ones that escaped loaded the coins aboard a ship that was ready to sail and threatened the crew on board to take off and they came to the new world. Thinking they had stolen gold coins, they were coming here and being rich. Those were the only coins stolen that were worthless, never recorded. This is all I can find, there is nothing else about the ship in my findings, I do coins, not ships, but I think what you have is those coins that were stolen."

We gathered all our things and thanked Professor Taylor, and I told him if I found the coins I would bring him a few for his collection.

In the next couple of weeks, I would go over to Mr. Henry's house and we would study. I kept wondering if the ship landed on the island I was on and what happened. Records showing ships leaving Ireland reaching the new world either landed or some sunk on the way, but only one was stolen that we found and no record of where it was going and if it ever made the trip. Now I had searched all I could and did not think I could gather any more information about that ship, my next search was to find my island. Now I knew where the coins came from. I told Henry Cook how much I enjoyed his company and what could I do to repay him. He told me this brought back life for him and he would like some of those coins so he could put them with his collections.

I started looking at maps again and figured I needed to look east, as thinking the ship would be coming from that direction. I knew how far a B61 float plane could travel without refueling, so charting on the maps I was going flying again. The next day I called to charter a plan for a half a day sightseeing, I could go the following Thursday morning. I was ready as I drove to the pier where the plane was to take off from. The pilot was an older man and I knew he had a lot of experience, so I told him where I wanted to look and off we went.

As we flew across the waters, the plane lifted up and I was praying this was my last search for the island I was on. We went straight east and I only noted very small islands, we went as far as we could go before returning back. I looked and looked but no luck. Upon returning I asked if we could go the following day, and he told me he already had a booking, but I could go inside and ask if the other pilot was available. I went to ask because I wanted to go more north next time.

"Friday's all booked but Saturday morning there is an opening with another pilot."

"Great, book it."

Friday I spent the day at the office checking on John and seeing how things were going. Saturday morning I awoke, had my breakfast and headed to the pier, when I walked through the gate this kid came up to me and wanted to know if I had an appointment for a float plane.

"Yes, well, my name is Jayden, I am your pilot. Do you want half a day or whole day, if you want a whole day I will grab some lunch for us."

"Where will you refuel if we do an all-day?"

"No need, I have a plane with a double fuel tank."

"I did not know they made two tanks on float planes, is this a special plane? Does anyone else have a plane like this. Did they have this thirty years ago?"

"Wow, you ask a lot of questions," Jayden said.

"Well, I need to know," so I told him I was rescued by a float plane and I needed to find out where I was when he found me.

"Well, it was about thirty to forty years ago, a guy invented this two-tank plane. He used to fly out in this area, they call it the B.B. fuel expansion tank. It is two equally dispensed fuel tanks located in the two float buoys, he invented it but through the years it was adjusted a little to make it safer. B.B. was the man who rescued me right before he was killed."

"Wow, I've heard stories about him. Sounded like a great guy."

I said I never met him or remembered meeting him because I was injured when he picked me up.

"Okay, let's go find an island," Jayden said.

"Here are the maps and where I have been, so let's go further east, then continue south since my search was limited on miles, now we can expand my search into new territory."

I told Jayden my sailing journey was heading east, but with the storm I did not know where after that. So we flew about three hours when I suggested we may go more south. I kept an eye on the islands we flew over but all were so small. He told me he had never been this far southeast.

"Let's give it fifteen more minutes, then we can head more south, then we need to circle back because high winds are expected this evening."

As we kept watch for a larger island we talked of our experience sailing, he loved to sail too, but flying was his true love.

"Let's head west and go back. Maybe the storm took me inward and we might find it as we head back."

About twenty minutes later l noticed an island covered with trees. "Jayden, can we take a closer look?"

"Your call," so we flew around the island, and there I saw large rocks peeking out of the water. "This may be the ones but the rocks are on the north side and I was on the east because the sun rise woke me up as it came over the water."

"Let's land so I can take a closer look."

"Not today, we have to get back before the weather hits."

I got the location, we can come back another time. Excited and upset, was that where my coins were hidden? As we landed the plane and got our stuff, we headed to the office when the rain started.

"Let's get a cup of coffee and I will chart the location and give it to you so if someone else takes you they will know where to go. It is about three and a half hours out, so my plane could take you if you wanted me to. We could land and I could look around to see if that is where I was."

"Alright, I will let you know if I need your plane."

When I got home I called John to come over. I was in the study when he arrived, so the three of us sat down and I showed them the map and the location of the island I thought I was on.

"So, how about the three of us sailing to this island and getting my treasure?"

"Wow," John said, "that will be like a ten-hour trip. Are you for sure this is the island?"

"Almost sure."

"But not certain," Laura said.

"No, we have to hurry. So do you want to take a chance and see?"

John said his boat was not big enough to go that far.

"I agree, and if we bring back all those coins we will need a bigger boat. How about if I take another flight and we can get a closer look and see if I can see the waterfall?"

We all agreed and if I was sure that was the island I was looking for we would all go.

The following Tuesday I called Jayden and booked a flight with him, so I made the appointment for Friday morning. When Friday finally arrived, we headed to hopefully what was my island. Once we got there I asked to fly as low as he could so l could spot the waterfall. We flew around and around, then I saw it, a waterfall.

"That is it!" I yelled. "Can we land?"

"No way I can land here, there are way too many rocks. How in the world did B.B. ever land his plane here? It is too dangerous and I am not taking a chance."

"Okay, I know this is it, let's go back home."

What a relief it was knowing that after all these years I had finally found where I was stranded. It was so peaceful flying back. I felt like my life had changed, no more worries, searching, daydreaming. It was over, now I needed to make a plan on how to get my treasure.

Now my plan to get my coins. I would need to rent a boat, one day there, two days to load the coins, one day back. Four days rental, great. I would need a wagon, to get the coins from the waterfall to the boat. I could put about forty to fifty pounds in a five-gallon bucket and carry it from the falls to the wagon, then to the boat. I figured six buckets loads per chest. With three chests that would be eighteen bucketloads and I could put three buckets in a wagonload. That would take six trips and each trip would take about three hours. I'd better rent the boat for five days, this would give us enough time.

August 14th, 9:00 A.M., was my rental date and time. With a little over two weeks before we took off, I had plenty of time to get the supplies together. During the time of waiting I had all the supplies stacked in my house. Laura seemed a little nervous because she never said it, but I knew she was thinking, what if the coins were not there? What would I do, where would I look, how would I react? She told me how proud she was that I never gave up on finding the treasure.

I kept going over my plan in case I overlooked anything, I was ready and confident it was going to go as planned. With two days to go we had everything stacked and ready, Laura had enough food to last us for the five days and John bought a tent with three blow-up mattresses for us to sleep on. We were ready to claim my treasure. John spent the night with us so we could get an early start.

That morning we loaded up all of our supplies and off we were. We stopped to eat breakfast so that would hold us for the day. As we came to the dock I kept a dolly in the pick-up, so when we came back we could load the buckets of coins onto the dolly so we could move them to my pick-up. I figured we would have no room in the boat for the wagon with the buckets of coins. I stacked the buckets inside one another to save space, but when they were full we would have to spread them out and the wagon would not fit. We had everything loaded by 9:30 and then we set sail. What a beautiful day. My calculations would put us on the island around 7:00 P.M., just before sunset. I thought we would use the wind to carry us but there was not much of a breeze, so I decided to use the motor so we would not lose any time. After about an hour and a half, the wind picked up and we raised the sails and away we sailed. Making good time, we just sat back and enjoyed the trip. We had a little snack around 4:00 and figured we had another 3 hours to go.

Then John yelled, "Land!" He could spot land through his binoculars and it looked to be about an hour away.

We put our stuff away and I let down the sails so we could use the motor, that way we could steer our way around the rocks. There it was, my island, my treasure, which I spent the last twenty-five years looking for. As we moved through the rocks we made it to the beach, where we anchored just off the beach. We unloaded our supplies and put the tent up, Laura was getting the food together to store it for the next five days. She thought the food that needed to keep cold we would eat first because the ice would only last for two days, then we would eat the canned foods and fruit she brought. Just as the sun was setting we were finishing up.

"What a sunset."

"Yeah, but wait until you see the sunrise."

After some walking around I said that when we woke up we would go towards the waterfall. I saw from the plane that it was just north of us and we could start carrying the wagon with the supplies and start collecting the coins. The stars were bright and we lay there talking, unable to go to sleep.

Before we knew it the sun was waking us up. We'd better eat some breakfast before we headed out, it was going to be a long hard day ahead of us, we'd better be ready for it. As soon as we ate we were off to the north, we walked and walked, then I heard it, water. The waterfall was straight ahead. I ran to the water and took off my shoes.

"Here, give me the rope, I will tie the pulley to this tree and I will take the other end through the falls and tie it to some rocks. This way I can pull the buckets towards you and you can send me an empty one."

I slowly eased my body into the water, it was cold, but my blood was pumping so fast it did not bother me much. When I went through the falls I tied the rope, and what l saw next was something I never dreamed of. No chest, my treasure was gone. Someone stole my treasure. I just knelt down and cried, then a rage came over me, I threw rocks, started screaming. I went crazy. Laura and John could not hear me over the falls but I totally lost it. I jumped through the falls and swam back.

"It's gone, my treasure is gone."

Laura said, "Maybe there is another fall, this might not be the one."

"It's the only one, I flew over this island and there is only this fall. Someone came and found the chest and took it." I just started walking, did not even put my shoes on, I just started walking back to the boat.

Laura and John were behind me and never said a word. They knew I was crushed.

John ran up to me and said, "Maybe a storm blew the chest into the pond."

"Well, that might have happened, let's see."

Laura said she was going to the boat and making dinner, we would be hungry this evening. So John and I went back to search the waters, hoping to find some coins in the bottom. We both jumped in and we looked and we looked. Nothing, we did not even find one coin, then we searched under the falls again, seeing if the thieves might have hidden some coins and would come back later to get them but no luck. They were gone.

We walked backed to the boat, where Laura was making dinner, her plan was to have a celebration dinner but instead a meal for the disappointed.

As I walked up to her I said, "My stomach is all in knots and I just can't eat right now." I lay down and cried myself to sleep.

I guess I passed out of a broken heart because the sunrise woke me up. We loaded up our stuff and headed back home. It was a quiet trip back home, no one really said much, there just wasn't anything to say.

For the next few days I did nothing but lie around, I didn't talk to anyone and I just shut Laura off completely, I was in my own world.

A couple of weeks later I received a phone call and Laura made me take the call, it was Professor Taylor, he told me that Henry Cook just passed away from a heart attack. He asked if I had any luck finding those coins that Mr. Henry really enjoyed looking up and searching for. I said I had no treasure and told him of my story. He said how sorry he was that I didn't find them, that I was so excited talking about them and what a disappointment it must be. He said, "GOD BLESS," as he hung up the phone.

As I hung up I thought that I was not excited now but what if that was the wrong island, most islands must've had waterfalls. Was I giving up too soon, was the island still there, was my treasure on another island, they all looked the same, I just didn't find the right island. I told Laura that I was going out and would be back later, she didn't ask where I was going, I'm sure she was glad for me to be out of the house. I drove to the airport to find Jayden and told him I wanted to go looking around for more islands, that if he could make room on his schedule to take me out two days a week until I found my treasure.

I stopped doing anything except searching for my treasure, John stopped calling and I never talked to Laura and after 6 months of me being so caught up in my search Laura left me. I was all alone but my search continued, and I was getting depressed and going broke all at the same time. One day while I was walking to the plane at the airport, I noticed a group of people and I asked this lady what was taking place there. She said that they were having a 30-year memorial for a man called B.B., he donated money to the airport and was a man who did a search-and-rescue for lost people that went sailing and had some type of trouble, she said that I would be surprised how many people he had saved and in his honor there was a plaque being put up. I walked over and someone asked if I knew him. I said I never meet him but he saved me, I was in a storm and was shipwrecked on an island and he found me, apparently I was the last person he saved. I woke up in the hospital six days later, during that time he was killed in a plane crash so I never got to thank him.

A gentleman walked up to me and said, "I remember you, I just started working in the emergency room when he brought you in. I remember he rescued you from a boat in the ocean, you had a piece of a wine bottle embedded in your foot, I thought how strange. The doctor and nurses worked really hard so you could keep your foot. I tried to get an IV started but you were so dehydrated that I couldn't, that is how I learned to make a stick from someone so dehydrated, I will never forget that. And with such a bad infection you would tell stories of an island, treasure chest and pirates, we talked about how you were talking out of your head for 5 days before the infections was cleared."

"Wait a minute, I was picked up out of a boat, not from an island."

"B.B. was searching for you after you were reported missing and found you floating around in a sailboat out in the ocean."

"How did B.B. get all his money?"

"Well, his sister said he was in the diamond business and made a lot of money, she said when they were small he dug up a box that was buried and in it was some old coins, not worth anything, just old. That is how he went and found some raw uncut diamonds and he just got into the business. He loved to dig for things and had a good collection of things he found, in fact, he made little boxes and he would put three old coins in them and he would give them to the ones he saved, just a way to cheer them up and know they were like those coins, being able to have a second chance. The gentleman said that was the last time he saw B.B., when he brought the little box of coins to you, but at that time you had not woken yet."

As I walked away, I thought all this time I was never shipwrecked on an island. I must have heard about the little box of coins and dreamed of me being on the island and finding a treasure chest of coins. I spent my whole life chasing a dream, I lost my family, my life. That is my Lost Treasure.

DON'T GO TO SLEEP

As I was putting on my shoes and finishing my first cup of coffee, I could smell bacon cooking. Laura, my wife, was cooking breakfast.

"John!" she yelled. "Breakfast is getting cold!"

Our 2 kids, Madison, who is 14, and Zoe, who is 10, just finished eating when I came to the table.

"Sorry I'm late, kids, I was getting all my papers together. Let me eat, then I will take you to school."

"Dad," Madison said, "you are coming to my football game today, aren't you?"

"Sure, at 5:00, right, but don't be mad if I am just a little late, I have to finish this ad for this guy so he can pick it up before 5:00 today."

I own an advertising company, which I call "John's Ad Company." Simple but catchy. Most of my business comes from our small island town and nearby towns, our town, White Sands, is connected by 2 bridges and is a summer vacation place. From April through September thousands of people come visit our town.

Laura said it might be halftime before she could make it. She said that they had 2 large deliveries of flowers this evening, Laura owned a flower shop and she had to deliver flowers to the funeral home, Mr. McGee's service was tomorrow.

"We have so many orders to fill, we will send one order today at 10:00 and the second at 4:00, but I will come straight to the game after that."

Zoe asked how old Mr. McGee was.

"89," I said, "and Monday through Friday he would walk from his house to the Chamber of Commerce office, where he helped with all the chamber activities. White Sands will be 150 years old next year and Mr. McGee was helping plan the event, he wanted it to be special. Every morning he would walk the 5 blocks from his house to the chamber, where he would make coffee and people would stop by and get a cup and talk to him. He was White Sands, all the visitors loved stopping by and getting information about the island and he was proud saying he was the longest-living person on the island, he was born here."

Madison asked how he died.

"He had a heart attack and died walking home from the chamber, just fell over on the sidewalk. Let's go, kids, you need to get to school and I need to go to work."

"Honey," said Laura, "you have to eat out for lunch today, I didn't have time to make your lunch."

"Alright, I will grab a sandwich and don't worry about dinner tonight, we can grab some hotdogs after the game and bring them home for dinner. That way if you need to go back to the shop and get ready for the funeral tomorrow, you don't have to worry about us eating."

"That will be great and sorry about lunch."

She makes me lunch 4 days a week and I eat out one day. Every week I put $40.00, which I save from eating out, into our vacation fund, which we use for spring break or summer vacation. We try to leave the island for vacation because everyone comes to White Sands.

As I gave Laura a goodbye kiss, she hugged me and told me how lucky she was to be married to me, I told her not to forget it either as the girls and I walked out the door.

On our way to the school Madison said, "Look, Dad, there is your ad you made, they are putting it up."

"Yes, they should be finished before lunch."

I have 3 billboards on the island and whenever I make a new ad for someone I put it up for one month to help advertise so everyone on the island will know and it is good marketing for my company. I made a deal with a sign company on the mainland to install the signs, everyone knows every 4 weeks new ads go up.

I pulled up to Madison's school and as she was getting out I told her, "Good luck at the game, I will be cheering for you."

Zoe's school was around the corner, and when we arrived I told her to have a good day and Mom was going to pick her up at 3:30 and she was going to the shop.

"Oh, Dad, love you."

Laura takes Zoe to work after school, where she does her homework and helps out when needed, Zoe loves flowers.

At work I called the insurance company to see if Bill could meet me for lunch so we could go over the new ad I had done for them. My one day a week eating out I try to take someone out for lunch. I've done ads for every business in White Sands and whenever I go into a business the people always tell me hello and usually shake my hand. New clients from the mainland find that very impressive and that helps me land that account. I am working on 4 other ads now and I try to keep in a timely matter so everyone will have my full attention as I work on their advertisement.

It was a busy morning and before I knew what time it was I looked up and saw it was 11:45, my luncheon was at 12:30 with Bill so I had to hurry and get everything together and head out. As I was driving by the school I was looking at the new ad that they just finished, at the 4-way stop I was thinking how excited Madison was this morning as she saw the new ad, she loved seeing those ads knowing that I designed them.

As I started driving a car ran the stop sign and plowed into me, that was what they told me at the hospital. I only remember waking up with Zoe Madison sitting on my bed beside me and saw Laura sitting in the chair crying.

"John, you're awake." She called the nurse and told them I was awake.

I asked, "What happened, how long have I been asleep?"

The doctor came in and told me I was in a coma for 3 days. He asked what was the last thing I remembered, and I told him eating lunch and driving, then nothing else. Laura hugged and kissed me with tears streaming down her face. Later they told my Laura stayed there night and day while I was in a coma, they didn't know if I was going to come out of it or not.

After 2 days of x-rays and tests I was moved out of ICU into a private room and the doctors seemed pleased with my recovery. He told me one more day of observation, then I could go home. After Laura and the girls left the hospital for the night I could not sleep, it was a restless night.

About 10:30 in the morning Laura came in along with the doctor.

"Well, John, I am letting you go home but let me know if you have trouble sleeping, I will call the hospital over at the mainland and have them do a sleep study, but everything looks good."

We told the doctor thanks for all they did and Laura gave him a hug, the doctor told me to take care of her, she was a good wife and I was a lucky man.

I told Laura, "Let's go get the girls from school and go get pizza for lunch."

"Alright," she said, "if you feel like it."

"You bet I do, I feel great."

We surprised the girls at school and we headed to our favorite pizza place, in fact that is the name of the business, "The Pizza Place," it was one of my ads which I named. At the table people came over and told me how glad they were to see me out of the hospital. As we left and walked to the car I was getting very tired, it was only a short distance to our house but it seemed longer. I went inside and told Laura I was going to take a nap and she said she was taking the girls to the store to buy some groceries, they wanted to make a special dinner for me tonight. She kissed me and off they went. I got into bed, how good it felt being in my own bed, I think I feel asleep as soon as my head hit the pillow.

When I woke up I was confused, the bedroom I was in was not mine, how did I get into someone else's bedroom? The last thing that I remember was going to sleep while Laura and the girls went to the store. As I walked of the bedroom into the living room I looked outside through the window, and there was an old van parked in the driveway. On the side of the van was a sign about animal grooming. I yelled for anyone in the house but nothing but silence, I then went out the front door and the street I was on was Hayes St. How did I get here? Nothing looked familiar, I put my hand in my pocket to get my phone but I remembered that when I went to bed I put it on my dresser. So I went inside to find a phone to call Laura. There in the living room was a pushbutton phone on the wall so I picked it up and called Laura, a recording came on which said that was not a working number. As I hung the phone up I noticed pictures, they were of me and this girl in this house, how could this be, I noticed a wallet on the table. I opened it up and saw a driver's license with my picture and the name Greg Wiley was on it. It was my picture and the name Greg Wily living at this address was on it, I fell to the floor and passed out.

When I awoke I was in my own bed, I heard Laura calling me saying that breakfast was ready, I walked down the stairs into the dining room, there was my family eating breakfast.

"Hey, sleepyhead," Laura said, "I need to hurry and get to work. I have to fill the orders for Mr. McGee's funeral."

"What are you talking about?" I said. "That was last week, before I had my accident."

"What accident, what are you talking about? You must have had some kind of dream."

Everything that was happening this morning was a repeat, Madison reminded me of her football game, Laura said she would be there before halftime and told me that I needed to eat out for lunch because she didn't have time to make me lunch.

"Hurry up, Dad," the girls said, they needed to get to school.

On our way to the school Madison said they were putting the sign up that I made, everything was just as it was before, I parked in front of Madison's school and told her I loved her and would be at her game, then I dropped of Zoe and told her I loved her as she got out of the car. I was in a daze all morning, that dream, it seemed so real, I couldn't stop thinking about it. While I was on the phone talking to a client and getting things ready for my luncheon, I was thinking about my accident.

"You better hurry or you will be late for lunch!" yelled my secretary from the other room.

"Alright, I am on my way,' I said.

On the way to the cafe I was scared driving, as I drove past the billboard they were just finishing it. I stopped at the 4-way stop, then carefully drove on, keeping my eyes open for anyone speeding through, nothing happened as I arrived at the restaurant and asked if Bill had arrived and they said he was sitting in the back, where it was quieter.

As I walked to the table Bill said, "Hello, John, glad to see you."

I said sorry that I was late, "it's been a crazy morning."

"No problem, just sat down right before you showed up," said Bill.

As we ate lunch and I showed him the ad, he was very excited and told me not to change anything, he loved it just like it was. We made plans to when I would have the ad ready and told him I would be putting up an ad on my billboard as I do with all my clients for 1 month, and usually it takes 3-4 weeks before it is ready to put up, so Bill asked if I could have everything ready in 6 weeks so he could start advertising then.

"Not a problem," I told him, and as we left the restaurant we shook hands and he told my now he sees why everyone loves doing business with me.

I said, "Thanks, we will keep in touch." I didn't think of my dream anymore.

At the office I was getting things ready for my 4:00 appointment, about the time I had all the papers laid out they showed up and 45 minutes later we were finished.

I got to the ballgame right at kick-off, Madison saw me and was waving to me. People around me were saying hello and "How's the family?" small-town talk. The 2nd quarter was almost over when Laura and Zoe came and sat by me, so we all got to watch Madison perform during halftime, they did a special cheer. As I watched Madison on the field, then I was looking at Laura and Zoe, I was thinking what a wonderful life I have here in White Sands.

After the game Laura had to leave and get back to work, so we stopped at the concession stand and bought hotdogs, Laura took hers with her to work and we took ours home. We try to help out the school activities and they make really good hotdogs. When we got into the car and were headed home Zoe was asking about Mr. McGee and his life, I told them he was born here, and we stopped at the park and I told them, "This is where the old school used to be, and right behind it was a house where Mr. McGee was born and lived his childhood."

So I drove 2 blocks over and showed them where he lived the past 60 years. I told them he never learned to drive, he walked everywhere or someone would drive him somewhere. Every day he would walk from his house past the area he was born and went to school to the chamber office.

So Zoe asked, "He walked this area, where he spent 89 years?"

"Yes," I said, "he loved this town and he loved telling visitors as well as the ones who live here the history of White Sands. His family came from Ireland to America and they ended up here. They were the first Irish to live here and have a business. His father was a butcher so they open up a meat market and then they added a coffee shop beside it. His mother was a great baker and she opened the coffee and tea house, where she sold baked goods. Back then people didn't have any way to keep meat cold, so they would buy just what they needed. He said they would go into the meat market and place their order, then go into the coffee house and drink tea or coffee and eat some of his mother's pastries."

"So," Zoe said, "it was like Starbucks."

"Well, yes, but way before its time."

"Did he have a wife and kids, and do they live here?"

"No, his oldest son was killed in the war and their youngest son died of a lung disease, neither were married. His daughter moved right after she graduated high school and went to college, then she got married and they moved here for 2 years, then they had a baby boy and she had problems with the delivery and she died when she gave birth. Her husband took the baby and moved off and never came back, so the McGees never got to see their grandson again. Mr. McGee's wife was cleaning a fish and had a fin go into her hand and it got infected, he would say her hand got so hot that when he would put ice on it, it melted in a matter of seconds. They took her to the hospital in the mainlands but she never recovered from the poison from the fish and she died 8 days later. She didn't have any family so this town was his family. When anyone would ask him how he was doing he would say, 'Very blessed to be living in this beautiful town.'"

As we got out of the car walking into the house, Zoe asked if there was anything she could do to help with the 150-year celebration since Mr. McGee was not here anymore. I said that was a great idea and I would take her to the chamber next Monday after school and find out what we could do to help.

When Laura came in she was worn out, so I made her a hot bath and placed a glass of wine beside the tub so she could soak and relax. I finished working on some papers I needed to finish. Laura came into the bedroom thanking me for the hot bath and wine, and she was telling me of all the flowers and plants, the funeral home is full. they have a board hanging up full of thank-you cards to Mr. McGee for all his help and his love. It was so sad that after the service there would be no one to take the flowers and plants. I told her I would talk to the funeral director in the morning and see if they could take everything to the chamber, that way the plants could keep in his memory and they could give the flowers to different people and businesses to enjoy in memory of Mr. McGee.

"That a great idea, thanks."

I told her of our talk this evening, about him and how Zoe and Madison wanted to help. She kissed me and said how blessed we were to have great girls, I said they took after their mother. With that came a big hug.

"Goodnight honey, I need to get some sleep," as I turned the light off she was already asleep.

When the alarm clock went off it scared me because I didn't set my alarm, Laura set hers. As I looked around I was dreaming again, I was back in the bedroom that I dreamed about before, no Laura, not my bed. I went into the living room, then into the kitchen. I walked through the hall into an empty bedroom. No one in the house, I went back to the living room and noticed that van still in the driveway. I walked out the back door to the backyard and this dog came running towards me, I ran into the house and the dog started howling, I opened the door and he started rubbing his head around my leg. I saw a bag of dog food so I filled his bowl with food and set it down on the patio. He started eating and never looked up. I went back into the house and looked around, I looked at the pictures with me and people I did not know. I saw some mail on the dining table and looked and they were all addressed to Greg Wiley. Then the phone rang, I picked it up and said hello.

A female voice said, "Good morning, Greg, how are you this morning?"

I asked, "Who is this?"

She said, "Greg Wiley, who do you think this is, I am in no mood in playing games, hurry you ass to work, people are waiting on you," then click.

I grabbed the wallet and looked at it again, Greg Wiley, born Jan. 15th, 1949, and expired 1977. I looked around the house trying to find something with a year on it when in the mail stack was a *Field and Stream* dated 1975. I went out to the van and looked at the tag, it was Texas with a 1975 sticker. I opened the glovebox and saw papers with Greg on them, I went to check the mailbox and they were addressed to Greg Wiley, walking back to the house there was a voice behind me saying, "Good morning, Greg." I turned and the woman across the street was waving at me, I waved back and went inside. I thought I would redial who called me this morning but when I picked up the phone it didn't have a way to call last caller, so I took a shower and put on some clothes in the closet that fit me perfectly. As I was putting my shoes on there was a knock on the door, so I hurried to the door when I fell.

"Wake up, honey, coffee is ready."

As I opened my eyes I was back, back in my bed and the voice was Laura. She brought me a cup of coffee and was about to walk out when she said that she had to go to work and do the last-minute delivery before the funeral at 1:00.

"Hey, Laura, what day is it?"

"It's Friday, are you alright?"

"Yes, just had a dream."

"Well, this is reality," she said, "get moving, don't want the girls to be late for school. I will meet you at 12:30 for the funeral."

So I got up and went to the bathroom, then was shaving, when I was looking in the mirror thinking I was shaving this same face with a different name in my dream, or now it was a nightmare.

As walked into the dining room I heard voices saying, "Good morning, Daddy," words that I love to hear.

"Morning, my angels, how is breakfast?"

"Sausage and pancakes, can't get any better than this," Zoe said.

Madison asked if I was going to pick them up after school, and I told them yes, then I would take them to the chamber. "All the stores in town will close from 12:00-3:00 today for the funeral, then after the services all the flowers and plants will be taken to the chamber so after school we all can help out there moving plants around, then we can deliver some to people around town in memory of Mr. McGee."

"That will be so much fun," they said.

"Alright, let me finish eating while you girls get your things ready for school, then we can go."

I only had a few things to do at work, so I thought I would talk to the funeral director and he thought that was a great idea and they would be glad to help. "I will have the van," I said, "and I can help, then my girls can help after school."

I went to pick up a couple of sandwiches for Laura and I so we could eat before the service. I left the office and picked up the sandwiches and got to the flower shop around 11:30. Laura was surprised and glad I showed up, and I told her that we could ride together because the parking lot would be full and we needed to be there before 12:30 if we wanted a seat. We barely found 2 seats together, it was packed with people standing in the overflow room and into the hallway. They said this was the largest crowd ever. The service lasted an hour and a half and was such a great honor to the man and of all his love, White Sands will miss him. He is the last McGee except for his grandson, whose last name is different and he will probably never know his mother's maiden name.

After the graveside Laura and I left to go get the girls, then I took Laura back to the shop and the girls and I went to the chamber. Ron, the chamber president, said how grateful he was for doing this. I helped with 2 vanloads of flowers while the funeral director brought the rest. The girls and I, along with Ron, put all the plants in front of the store and loaded some flowers in the van. We went to different stores and handed out the flowers so everyone could enjoy them.

When we drove back to the chamber it was beautiful with all the flowers, he said he sure would miss him.

"So will everyone else," I said.

The girls asked if there was anything they could help with to get ready for the 150 celebration.

Ron said, "Life goes on, so let's go into the office and we can go over what we have so far."

As we all sat at the conference table Ron brought in a huge notebook.

"This is White Sands history. Next March on the 17th, which is St. Patrick's Day, is the 150-year of White Sands, they never knew exactly what month it was established but in 1895 Mr. McGee's father set a 25th anniversary on the 17th of March, being from Ireland, seemed okay for everyone living here at that time, so 3-17-1825 is the date the town was established, so we celebrate with a parade St. Patrick's Day as well as the anniversary of White Sands. It's getting late and if you want to come after school Monday we can see what all there is to do, we only have 5 months to go, and we want to make this special."

On the way to the flower shop, we left the van and told Laura we were going to the store and we were going to cook her dinner tonight. The girls love to help me cook since I can only grill and they help with the rest. When Laura came in the girls had a beautiful salad made with potatoes in the oven, I was grilling steaks outside. Zoe came outside and asked if we could put a fence in the back of the yard since we have the side fenced. I asked why.

"Well," she said, "one of my friends has a dog that is about to have puppies and she said I could have one."

Just as she was talking about puppies in the backyard, I remembered that dream and the dog in the backyard.

"Daddy, are you listening to me, can I have one, please?"

"Well, Zoe, I need to think about this, having a dog is a lot of responsibility."

"I know, Daddy, we will feed it, play with it, keep the yard clean, I promise."

I told her I would talk to her mother about it.

As we were sitting at the table enjoying our meal, my mind was on that dream. That dog at the house I was in, I just couldn't understand why I was having that dream over and over. The girls were telling Laura about the chamber and how they were going to help with the 150-year anniversary. We all talked for a while, then the girls helped with the dishes. After everything was cleaned up the girls went to their room to watch a movie, while Laura and I sat in the living room. I was reading a book and Laura was talking to her friend on the phone, but it didn't take long until I was drifting to sleep and I kept reading the same thing over, so I told Laura I was going up to the bedroom and go to bed. She told me she would be there shortly.

As I got into bed and lay down, getting comfortable, Laura came and got in bed with me and she gave me a kiss and said, "Sweet dreams."

I said, "I hope so," and turned out the light and went straight to sleep.

The next thing I knew was the light coming through the blinds, lying there I was thinking I must have slept late, as I reached over to touch Laura she had already had gotten up. As my eyes opened I looked and "oh, no" I was back in the bedroom in my dream. I got out of bed and walked into the kitchen, there on the table was a box of donuts with a note on it saying, "Good morning, hope you are feeling better, call me when you wake up and enjoy your donuts. Love, Shelby." Who is Shelby and why did she bring donuts? I made some coffee and sat at the table drinking coffee and eating donuts, wondering how long it would be before I woke up. I thought I needed to see who this Shelby person is, so I looked around for an address book and I found a phonebook with names and addressed written in the back of it. So I dialed Shelby's number and this voice answered, saying how was I feeling and how was my head.

"Okay, I guess, did you bring me donuts?"

"Well, who else would and leave a note saying 'Love, Shelby'?"

I asked if she could come over, I needed to talk to her, she said she just finished washing her hair and as soon as she was dressed she would be over.

"Okay," I said, and hung the phone up.

I decided to take a shower and wake myself up and see what that would do. After a good hot shower I was still here and I went to the closet and put on some clothes, they all fit me perfectly, if this was the 70s people really knew how to dress.

As I went out to the backyard to see that dog was still there and sure enough there he was, so I fed him, then I heard a voice inside the house saying, "I'm here." As I walked into the house there stood this girl saying, "Hi, baby," and she gave me a kiss and a hug.

"Shelby," I said.

"Wow, you must have fell hard, at least you know my name, let me look at your head, last night you still had a knot on it."

I asked if she was here last night. Yes, but I was out of it, Ron went to pick up something to make me relax.

"So we kept ice on your head until the swelling went down and gave you the pills and I went to sleep fast."

"I don't remember anything."

"Well, Ron came over yesterday and when he knocked on the door he heard a loud noise, so when he opened the door there you were lying on the ground with a big bump on your head, so Ron called me and when I came in he had ice on your head, hoping to get the swelling to go down. He called Dr. Taylor and he said to keep a close watch on that bump and if the ice didn't make it come down to bring you into the hospital, he was going to call some medication to help with the pain.

So Ron picked up the medication and I made some potato soup for you and gave you an RC Cola, then I gave you the pills and took you to bed. I gave you a kiss and told you goodnight and you didn't say anything, you were so sleepy and you went to sleep before I turned out the lights."

"Wow, listen, I need to tell you something, and please just listen and don't say a word and don't get mad, just listen, please. First of all, this is not my life. I don't know who I am or where I am. I am in a dream from the year 2020, where there I am married and I have 2 girls. Every time I go to sleep I wake up here, in this house, but each time this dream picks up where it left off. Shelby, are we dating? If so how long? What town is this? Is this my house?"

Shelby said that I was scaring her and even though it was Saturday she was getting hold of Dr. Taylor and telling him what I told her and what should she do.

"All I need is to wake up. I don't need a doctor."

"Greg, you are awake, you're talking to me but just not making any sense. Let me call Ron."

"Who is this Ron?" I asked.

"He is your best friend, you went to school together and play in a band sometimes. Listen," she said, "why don't we go ride around town and go to Ron's house, maybe something will jar your memory."

I agreed to go for a ride and as we walked outside I asked if that van was mine.

"Yes," she said, "and the sign on the side, 'Groovy Tails Dog Grooming, is your business, that is what you do for work." Shelby told me I was the one who trained dogs and my 2 employees Dayton and Sky did all the grooming. "Does any of this sounds familiar?" She said, "We have been dating a few months," and she was waiting for me to pop the question, she gave me a long, hard kiss and asked if that brought back my memory.

I said, "Sorry, but no."

"Jump in my car and let's explore Blue Rock."

"What is Blue Rock?" I asked.

"It's where I spent the last 26 years." She said I was born here. Ron and I were best friends and grew up together. I asked if my parents were here and Shelby said, "Let's just go to Ron's house, there we can tell you more."

As we drove through this little town there was my business, Groovy Tails, but it did not ring a bell. As we passed the school I noticed a big sign, "1966 Football State Champions."

"Wow, they must had a good team, state champions."

"Yes, Greg and you were the wide receiver and safety. Ron was the quarterback and you were great together."

"I never played football," I said.

"Here you did and you were good."

We pulled into a drive and this guy came over and said, "Hi there, good buddy."

As I heard the door close I jumped up, I heard Laura say, "Sorry for waking you, I didn't mean to." I just looked at her and she said, "It's 8:45, I slept until 8:00 myself. The girls just woke up and they are eating cereal. Why don't we pack a lunch and all go to the lake today, it's beautiful outside. John, does that sound good?"

I said, "Let me have some coffee first, I need to wake up."

Laura looked into my eyes and asked if everything was alright. I just said I had a strange dream again. She asked what did I mean again.

"Never mind, let me get my coffee."

As I sat at the table the girls were washing their bowls and asked if we were going to the lake. I said alright and they gave me a hug and said how much they loved me. I told them to get dressed and I would do the same, then we could pack and go to the lake. I knew this would take my mind off of this nightmare I just had.

Laura came in and started making sandwiches, cutting up some fruit and making lemonade. We were all outside loading up the van, I put the fishing gear in while Laura put the food in. We all got in the van and I started off, there is this one place not many people went to and hopefully no one would be there. I told the girls that we would stop at the bait store and get some shrimp, I heard the catfish were biting on shrimp. I picked up a bag of ice and I put the frozen shrimp on the floor. Laura said not to get shrimp on the floormat. She didn't want her flowers to smell like shrimp. The girls laughed and I said they were frozen and wouldn't thaw out before we got there.

When we arrived we were lucky and no one was there, so I parked and we all unloaded everything. I sat up the table and chairs. The girls went to the edge of the water to get a good look and I told them not to get too close, that was about a 20-foot drop and the water was too cool for me to go jumping in to rescue the 2 of them. They took their chairs and fishing poles to the edge, and I brought my gear and put the shrimp on their hooks and the fishing had started. Zoe asked if we caught enough fish could we eat them tonight, "Sure thing," I said. It took about 15 minutes before Madison got a bite, I told her to jerk the rod and start reeling, just as she did her pole bent and she was hanging on.

"Reel," I said.

She was doing her best but the fish was really pulling, I helped her hold the rod as she reeled, I grabbed the net and when she finally got it close I used the net to get it. What a beauty, 25 inches long, "What a big fish," she said.

Zoe yelled, "Daddy, your pole is moving!"

I pulled back and I had a fish, it was also a big one, as I pulled it to the shore Zoe said she had one, I was netting mine while Madison helped Zoe and when I used the net to get hers we had 3 nice fish. With all the action Laura came down to see what was going on.

Zoe said, "Look, Mom, dinner."

Laura said we could eat in about an hour so we fished until then, where we caught plenty for dinner, and when we walked up to where Laura had lunch ready Zoe and Madison both said how much fun that was.

Laura said, "Wash your hands really good and come eat."

After a relaxing lunch the girls wanted to go look for fossils, I said, "Alright, but be careful."

Laura sat in her chair and she wanted to finish ready her book while I sat in my chair enjoying the warm sun.

I must have dozed off when I heard someone say, "Greg, how are you?"

"How long have I been here?"

"You and Shelby just walked in, are you alright?"

"No, I am not alright. I just awoke from a nap where my wife and 2 daughters were fishing and having a picnic."

"Hey, man," he said, "sit down and tell me about it."

"Are you Ron?" I asked.

"Yes, I am, your best friend, and that is why you are going to tell me what is going on."

I told him I don't remember anything about this town. "I am from White Sands in the year 2020. I am in this dream where I end up here every time, then I wake back up at home in 2020."

"Man, you must have got into some bad pot."

"I don't do drugs," I said, "at least in 2020 I don't."

Ron said, "Let's call Dr. Taylor and ask if we can come over."

"Who is Dr. Taylor anyway?"

"You know, it's Derek's dad."

Again I said, "Who?"

"Derek, our drummer in our band, his dad, who's been your doctor since you were born."

I said, "This is all confusing, can I use your phone? I need to call my wife."

He said, "It is in the kitchen."

So when I dialed Laura's phone it was a non-working number, so I tried my cell and the same results. I told them I tried my wife's cell and my cell but not a working number.

Shelby asked, "What is a cell?"

As I looked on the wall there was a calendar, October 1975. I just stared when Ron said, "Let's go to Dr. Taylor's office." I looked at Shelby and she had tears in her eyes, saying she was scared. Ron said, "Let's go," he would drive.

Shelby and I got into the back seat, where she hugged me tight and started crying on my shoulder. When we arrived at the hospital we went inside, where Dr. Taylor was waiting. The nurse told us to go into room 3 and the doctor would be right in. We walked into this big room and we sat. When this doctor came, he shook my hand and said, "Hello, Greg, good to see you." He told me he wanted to tape record our conversation and I agreed. He said, "Let's start from the beginning, tell me everything from as far back as you can remember."

I said, "In 1975 or 2020?"

He looked puzzled and said, "Now, in 1975."

Well, that didn't take long and he asked if that was all I could remember and I said yes. Now in 2020, which took much longer and after a while he told me to get to when I started having this dream.

"I stopped when I was taking a nap after fishing, and this is where we are now."

He stopped the recording and said, "We need to take a break, would you like a soda or something?"

I said, "Just a bottle of water."

"What?" he said.

"Water."

He had the nurse bring me a glass of water.

"Look, Greg," he said, "I want to do some tests but not here, I want to send you to Family Medical, they have more equipment in which we are needing. I have a doctor friend and I want to talk with him and we can do the testing to find out what is going on. Let me get a hold of him while you just sit here and wait."

Ron and Shelby just sat there not saying a word. It wasn't long until he came back and said it was all set for Monday, would that be okay? I said, "If I am still here I will go, but I can't make any promises," and Dr. Taylor said if I was in 1975 please be at the hospital.

Shelby let out a cry and I hugged her and said, "I don't where or who I will be Monday morning. Please don't cry, I know we must have been close."

"Close?" she said. "We love each other, why can't you remember that?"

"Alright, let's just calm down," said Dr. Taylor, "why don't you stay at Ron's house until Monday morning, then I can come and pick you two up and we will go and run some tests? Or maybe you would feel better if I just admitted you to the hospital for the weekend so we can keep an eye on you."

"No way," said Shelby, "we are going to his house and I will keep my eyes on him and try to make him remember us. I love you, Greg, and I will try my best to bring your memory back to this time and this place."

"Okay then, Shelby, would you wait here while I talk to Greg outside, just need to tell him something personal and I will be right back."

As we went outside Dr. Taylor told me that this was so strange and for me not to get upset at Shelby, she just wanted me back. He told me to wait and he would go get her and we could go back home.

When he walked into the room to get Shelby, he told her to watch me closely and to give me these pills, but dissolve them in tea, coffee or a soda, and don't let me know because I was afraid to go to sleep but these pills would help me go into a deep sleep and I needed to relax.

As we drove home no one hardly said a word, Ron parked the car and Shelby said she was taking me home to rest this weekend.

"Call me if you need anything," Ron said.

"Will do, thanks for the ride," and she gave him a hug.

As he drove off he gave me a peace sign and I just waved back.

"Okay, baby, let's go, I am going to take you home to make you a dinner you will never forget. What are you hungry for?"

"Well, how about fajitas, that sounds good."

Shelby looked at me and asked, "What are fajitas?"

"I forgot that fajitas weren't popular in 1975, hey, about a homemade pizza?"

"Great, pizza it is."

She said she needed to get some gas and go by the store first, I told her okay.

As we drove to the gas station this guy came to the window and asked, "What will it be?"

She said, "$10.00 on regular."

I just watched as this guy started pumping gas, then he cleaned the window and checked the oil.

"Ten dollars," he said, and Shelby gave him the money and off we were to the store.

I was still in amazement at watching that, I totally forgot about full-service stations.

She got out at the store and came to my side and asked if I would come in with her.

"Alright," I said, and we walked inside and she started picking up some items for the pizza. She asked if I had any red wine at home, I said, "I have no idea." She just stood there staring at me with a tear in her eye and said she was sorry for asking that question. "I will get some anyway," she said, and we checked out and drove home.

When walked inside the house she told me to go sit in the living room and watch some television while she was making the pizza. As I sat I was looking around for the remote control but didn't find it. Shelby came in and asked what was wrong, she didn't hear the TV playing, I told her I couldn't turn it on. She walked over to the TV and pushed a button and on it came.

"I guess you didn't push it hard enough."

"Guess not," I said.

So I walked over to change the channels and it was very limited on channels, I found "The Mod Squad" on so I watched that and watched two more old shows, well, in 2020 they are old, as Shelby made dinner. I kept wondering if I went to sleep, where would I wake up? Then she said, "Come eat," I went into the dining room and there she had two glasses of wine and a big salad. "The pizza is almost done," so she said, "let's have the salad first. If you don't mind I wish you would tell about your dream so I can understand more, but I want details, please."

I told her everything about my growing up, getting married and having 2 girls. I knew it was hard for her to listen but she wanted it. I told her of my life in 2020 and as I kept talking she kept listening, we finished our dinner and our wine so she opened another bottle. While we drank another glass I was finishing up my life story as I left it, "and now I am here."

"Wow, if this is real then hopefully Monday we can have an answer."

I knew she was looking for my memory to return, but how could I tell her that this was my dream, now, not dreaming about 2020? So I would not say anything and would just see what happened. I might as well enjoy my life here and make the best of it.

She got up from the table and went into the kitchen and told me to go take a shower but first she had something for me, as I waited there she brought me a cup.

She said, "Here is some flavored coffee, you favorite, coconut with rum."

Now she told me to drink it and then take a shower while she cleaned the kitchen and got ready for bed. I drank the coffee, which was really good, then went to shower and after that I crawled into bed and was kind of excited but again nervous about sleeping with Shelby, I was married in my real life but this was just a dream. I must have went to sleep before she got into bed because the next thing I remembered was a dog barking. I thought I was back home so I rolled over and put my arm around Laura's back, but my arm was laying on long hair and Laura's hair is not long.

"Good morning, My Love."

I opened my eyes and—OH, NO—it was Shelby, I didn't wake up from my dream, I was still dreaming.

She said, "Hey, you are awake and you are here, maybe that dream is over and we can just lay here all day long, we have nothing else to do today."

I asked, "What day is it?"

"Well, it's Sunday," she said, "remember, we go take tests in the morning. That darn dog, I am going to go feed Sam so he will stop barking."

I asked, "Who is Sam?"

She said, "Sam is your dog and he won't stop until he is fed. Now stay here and I will be right back."

I told her to make some coffee, I needed some.

"Okay," she said.

As she got out of bed she was naked, I thought, what have I done? I didn't remember anything after I took a shower. She turned toward me and said that I was out of it because I never once touched her, I felt such a relief but never told her that, I only said it must be the wine. She laughed as she put on a robe and left the room.

While I drank a cup of coffee the phone rang and Shelby answered.

"Hey, it's for you, it's Sunshine," so I got up and went to the phone.

"Hello?"

"Hey, boss," she said, "I know it's Sunday but we have a problem at the store, can you come down here?"

I asked what problem was it and she said that dog "Doc" was going crazy.

"I was bathing him because they are picking him up in the morning and he went crazy on me. I really need your help."

Shelby asked what was the matter and I told her, "But I don't know anything about dogs."

Shelby grabbed the phone and told Sunshine we would be there after we dressed. "Look," she said, "you are great with dogs, now let's get dressed, maybe you can remember something."

After we got ready she said she would drive us in the van, "Where are the keys?" She stopped for a second and said, "Let's look for the keys," and they were on the table under the mail. We jumped into the van and she drove to "Groovy Tails." When we walked in there was this girl all wet.

"Here," she said, "take him," and she handed me his leash.

Everything was good until I started bathing him, I started petting him, rubbing his neck and head. I said, "He has a fear of water, you have to rub him with wet towels and don't let him get close to water."

How did I know that?

I took him out back and was giving him commands, and he was calm and I walked around with him, then I went inside and put him inside his pen.

"Well done," said Sunshine, "didn't know he had a fear of water."

"Neither did I."

"Hey, baby, you remembered," said Shelby.

So she told her of my memory loss and I was having tests done tomorrow.

"Well, tomorrow is pretty easy, Dayton and I can handle it. Just let me know if Dayton and I can do anything."

"I will," I said as we walked out.

Shelby said, "I am hungry, let's stop for breakfast."

"Okay, you are the driver."

We stopped at the Blue Bonnet Cafe for breakfast. As we walked in and sat at a table some people said, "Morning, Greg," so I returned the greeting, not knowing who I was talking to. We ordered pancakes with bacon and coffee.

As I sat there eating my pancakes, I couldn't help but to remember when Laura made us pancakes right before we went to the lake.

Shelby said, "Let's go back to the house if you are ready."

"I am finished," I said.

Shelby asked if I felt like changing clothes and going to the beach. I told her she could go, I just wanted to go to the house.

"That's cool," she said, "I will just lay out in the backyard and get a tan."

On the way back I asked questions about the town and those people at the cafe but nothing seemed familiar, but why should it, I was in a dream. But how did I know about that dog, this was all too much.

She stopped by her house to grab her bathing suit, then back home. After we arrived back at the house Shelby changed into her suit and took a lawn chair into the back and laid out to get some sun. I sat out on the deck watching her, wondering if this nightmare would ever end, I sat there as Sam laid beside my chair. I must have dozed off.

"Hey, Daddy."

As I opened my eyes to see who was talking to me, Zoe was asking if I had talked to Mom about the dog.

Laura spoke out, "What is this about a dog? Zoe said she had asked about fencing the back part of the yard to put a dog in."

I was back.

Laura said, "Zoe, you know how I feel about a dog, it's a lot of responsibility to take care of an animal. Now let's load up, your dad has fish to clean."

So I put the fish in baggies, then into the ice chest, I didn't want the van to smell like fish. After everything was loaded off we went home, on the way I told Laura that we had plenty of fish, why didn't we call Jaxon and Trinity to come over for a fish fry tonight?

"That is a great idea," she said, and would call them when we got home.

When we got home the girls unloaded the van while I took the fish out back to clean them. Laura was talking to Trinity when I came inside and she said they were coming, Laura said not to bring anything, we had everything. I thought maybe I could talk to Jaxon about my dream, I knew he would keep it a secret. We had been friends since grade school.

I went upstairs to take a shower and get into some clean clothes. Laura already changed and was cooking potatoes for the potato salad when I walked into the kitchen. I said I was going to clean off the deck and the girls could put a tablecloth on the table and set the table. Just as I finished I heard Jaxon and he came outside with a sack of beer.

"Where can I put these, John?"

I said, "Put all of them in the cooler but keep two out for us."

"Will do," he said.

"Hey, let's sit over here, I need to tell you something but I don't want anyone else to know."

"Okay, what is it, John?"

"Well, I've been having a dream, whenever I go to sleep I wake up in a dream. I wake up in 1975, a little town in Texas. I live there and I have a business and a girlfriend. Everyone knows me there and my name is Greg. Then when I go to sleep there I wake up here. Always exactly where I left off, I wake up in the other place where I fell to sleep."

"Wow, John, how long has this been going on?"

"Ever since my accident."

Jaxon asked, "When did you have an accident?"

"I dreamed I was in an accident, it was Thursday before Mr. McGee's funeral, Madison was cheering at the football game that night. But that was a dream because I woke up. It was a dream inside a dream, because I took a nap when I came home from the hospital and I woke up in 1975. Apparently I fell in my dream in 1975 and I hit my head and I woke up here the morning I dreamed I had an accident, except that day I never had the accident, it's like that day never happened but it seemed so real. Ever since then whenever I fall to sleep I wake up in another time, sounds crazy, doesn't it?"

"John, that is really weird, I don't know what to say."

I said, "Please do me a favor, look up Blue Rock in Texas and see if there is a place, I am going to look up this Greg Wiley and see if he is a real person. And don't tell Laura yet, I don't want to scare her, let's do some research first."

"Fish is ready, we will bring it outside."

As we all sat there the girls told of how we caught the fish, it was funny because each one caught the biggest fish. Jaxon said that they were true fisherwomen. After we finished eating and cleaning the kitchen and the deck, Trinity said she needed to get home and she had some work she needed to do. She said she was giving a speech Monday to the new employees on their policy and procedure at the hospital. She told us thanks for the fish and as always there were thankful for friends like us.

As they left the girls came and gave me a goodnight hug and said they were going to watch a movie in their room. So Laura and I sat in the living room to watch a movie and on AMC was a classic, *Jaws*, it just started so we watched the entire movie and I told Laura, "Let's just sit here a little longer," and *Rocky* was coming on and Laura said she didn't care for *Rocky* but I asked if she would just cuddle with me while I watched it and she agreed. Within 30 minutes Laura fell asleep but I kept watching, hoping I could stay awake all night, I was struggling to keep awake but apparently gave in and fell asleep.

I felt something licking my hand, it was Sam. I looked around and no one was here. I went into the house and heard the shower running.

As I walked closer Shelby said, "Babe, why don't you join me?" but I told her my head was hurting.

She said for me to take two of those pills that the doctor gave me, she would be out in a minute. I asked what were the pills for, she said it was to calm my brain, so I wouldn't worry so much. Great, I thought, maybe I could go to sleep and wake up back home. So I grabbed a root beer and took two pills, then sat on the couch. Then the doorbell rang and Shelby ran to answer it, thinking I was asleep. It was Derek and she said come in.

"Hey, Greg, you okay? When you didn't show up for band practice I tried calling but it was busy."

"That was me," Shelby said, "I thought Greg was sleeping and didn't want him to wake up so I took the receiver off the hook."

"Sorry to wake you, man, just checking."

"That's okay, I had a headache and needed to relax."

"I will be going. I will tell the guys to skip practice tonight and we can hook up next week, that cool?"

Shelby closed the door and came and sat down beside me and I told her, "Who was that Derek guy?"

"He is in your band," she said, and I was the drummer.

"Wow, this Greg sure has a lot more talent than I do in 2020. He was a star football player, plays in a band, has his own business and a beautiful girlfriend, must be very popular."

"He is, I mean, you sure are, I especially like the girlfriend part," as she kissed me. "Sit here and watch television and I will make you a sandwich, we can just relax until we go to bed and be ready to go to the hospital in the morning. Look in the *TV Guide* and see what time the NBC movie premier of *Jaws* is coming on, I heard people that saw it at the theater and they said it was scary."

As Shelby came and brought us a sandwich we sat in front of the TV and watched *Jaws*, just as Laura and I did only hours ago.

After the movie ended Shelby said, "Let's go to bed and I will set the alarm for 6:45, then I will go home and change, then come back and pick me up."

As I lay there being very still, pretending to be asleep, I didn't want her to know I was awake, no telling what would happen. I closed my eyes and wondered where I would wake up.

"Honey, wake up, John, we feel asleep on the couch, let's go to bed."

Thank God I was back home, but I couldn't go to sleep. Laura was tired so I would just lay there until she fell asleep, then I would get up and not go to sleep. She was sound asleep within minutes so I went into the kitchen and started writing down everything in my dream or dreams. It was 3:15 and I was still writing, it was about 5:30 when I finished everything so I went into the garage and put them in my car so I could take them over to Jaxon in the morning.

Trinity had to work in the morning so I was going over to Jaxon's and we were going to do some research. I went back inside and made coffee and drank coffee and sat out on the deck just thinking when Laura came out here with her cup.

"How long have you been up?" she asked.

"Just a little while." I told her I was going to Jaxon's house, he bought a new grill and needed help putting it together.

"Okay." She said that her and the girls were going to the mall to buy some clothes and I told her to have fun.

I got out of the car at Jaxon's house and had my notebook with me, as I rang the doorbell he opened the door and said, "Come in, John, let's get some coffee and sit at the table, I already have the laptop there ready to go. Trinity won't be home until 3:15 or so. Okay, where do you want to start?"

I said, "Blue Rock."

As he searched there it was, Blue Rock in South Texas, population 7538, a small town named after a river and the bluffs, the color of the water was so blue and was surrounded by large rocks so they called the town Blue Rock in 1878.

"Looks like a normal small town in Texas, a hospital, funeral home, churches, stores, car dealership, schools, no large companies."

I asked if there were pictures of the town but not many.

"They have a library and history museum, a lot about the schools, you know football in Texas."

I said, "Look and see if they were state champions in 1966."

"Yes, in 1966, 1971, and 1980. How did you know to look that up?"

"Because Greg Wiley played on the 1966 state champion team."

"That's crazy, John."

"Look and see if there are any names listed with the teams."

"No names," he said.

"Look up Greg Wiley, can you find that name?"

After looking no name showed up, not many names, just information about the town.

"How far of a drive is it from here?"

"Looks like about a 16-hour drive. Why, are you thinking about driving there?"

"How about a road trip?"

"John, what would you tell Laura? When are you going to tell Laura?" he said.

"Soon. Let me think about this, in the meantime where is that grill?"

We worked on the grill until we finally finished it, never seen so many bolts and screws, but it was finished. On my way to the car Jaxon walked me and told me that Laura needed to know and I needed to tell her soon.

"I will," I said, and I got into the car and was on my way home.

I knew I had to tell her but I didn't want her to get hurt or mad at me for dreaming of a girlfriend. I went inside and they were still shopping, so I sat down and watched football. About an hour later the girls came in and started showing what they had bought.

"Look," said Madison, "Mom and me are going to make my mum today, that's right, next Thursday is homecoming and look at my dress."

"How beautiful," as I looked over at Laura.

"No, this is her first homecoming and we have to go all out. Okay, girls, go put everything in your rooms."

"Hey, Laura, we need to talk, I have something to tell you."

"Alright, let me get a glass of water and I will be right back. Okay, what is it you want to talk about?"

"Let's go out on the deck so the girls won't hear us."

"Oh, John, you are scaring me."

"It is scaring me too," I said.

So I told her of my dreams, my accident, my waking up in 1975, then again here, then back there.

After I finished telling her everything she just stared at me. "So John, you dream of another life, is that what you are wanting, another life?"

"No," I said, "it is a past life. I wake up there, then I wake up here, I don't know what to do."

"Well, I know what we are going to do," she said, "we are going to see Jayden. I am calling him tonight and see when he can talk to you."

I told Laura that he is really busy on Mondays at the clinic.

"John, he and McKennsie are our friends, let me call him tonight and tell him what is going on, he will probably talk to you tonight, I don't want to wait any longer to find out what this is all about."

"Okay, honey, let me call him now."

"Daddy, come and look at my dress, I just put it on for you."

As I went into the house I saw my little girl in a dress that made her look so grown up. "You are so beautiful, Madison, you will be the prettiest one out there, I feel sorry for the other girls, they don't have a chance."

She gave me a big hug and said thanks.

I went upstairs to the bedroom so I could have some privacy and call Jayden. I was remembering how I told Taylor in my dream about the same thing, this was way too much. I sat on the bed and called my friend, Jayden answered the phone and I asked if he had time to listen to my strange dreams that kept on going. He told me he had as long as I needed, so I started from the beginning and ended up at this moment.

"Wow," Jayden said, and asked if I had any headaches or blurry vision.

I said, "No, but my head feels so mixed up, thinking that if I go to sleep I don't know where I will wake up."

Jayden told me he wanted me to come into the hospital in the morning at 7:00 and he would meet me there in the waiting room. "I want to run a scan on your brain and see if there is anything that may be causing you to feel this way. I will be busy at the clinic but will have them call me as soon as the image is complete. Have Laura come by after she takes the girls to school and she can wait with you until I get over there."

I told him thanks and I would be there in the morning. "Laura and I are frightened and I wonder if I have a mental issue or something."

Jayden said, "Let's don't get ahead of ourselves, we will do a scan first and go from there, I will see you in the morning, try and get some sleep."

"Sleep, that is the last thing I need, I might wake up in 1975."

"Whatever happens I will see you in the morning."

I was walking downstairs and thinking how strange, I was having tests done tomorrow when in my dream I was also having tests run, maybe I would find the answer tomorrow, somewhere.

As I walked into the kitchen I asked, "What are you cooking?"

"Pasta, salad and garlic bread."

"Sounds good and smells even better." I told Laura about my talk with Jayden and the plans for in the morning. "I think I will go into the living room and watch some football."

"Okay, I will bring you a plate as soon as it is ready."

"Never mind, I will pause the game, I want us to eat together at the table. I can watch the game later after we eat, I will probably stay up tonight, I don't want to go to sleep."

Laura looked at me and said, "Okay, then you can do the dishes."

"Done deal," I said.

As the girls came down they sat the table and came to get me and said dinner was ready. We all sat down and it was Zoe's turn to say the blessing, which she loved to do. As we started eating the girls asked what time we were going to the chamber tomorrow.

I said, "Tomorrow might not be a good day to go because I am going to be busy, but we will go the next day if everything goes okay tomorrow."

So we talked about the anniversary, school, cheerleading and homecoming. I just listened to the girls talk and held Laura's hand and told her how lucky I was to have a family like this.

The girls looked at us and said, "We love you, Daddy and Mommy."

"Tonight is my turn to clean the table and do the dishes, now you two go get your schoolwork ready for tomorrow and get ready for bed. And you, my sweetie, go take a relaxing bath and get some sleep."

"I will," she said, "but after my bath I will come down and we can watch a movie on the couch."

"Sounds good," I said, "I will make some coffee and clean the kitchen until you come down."

I just finished washing the dishes when Laura came into the kitchen and poured us coffee.

"Come on," she said.

We sat on the couch and found a movie, *The Notebook*, Laura's favorite. We sat there watching the movie and drinking coffee, and as the movie was coming to the end I saw tears coming down her cheek, she looked at me and said she hoped we will be together when we are that old.

"Me too," I said, and gave her a hug.

After it went off she said she was going to bed.

"I am going to watch that football game."

Laura gave me a kiss and said goodnight and she would set the alarm for in the morning.

It was about 1:45 when the game ended, so I went into the kitchen and swept the floor and took out the trash. The cool air outside made me wide awake, so I decided I would watch another movie, I found one of my favorite movies, *The Time Machie*, it was just starting. I watched the movie and thought about time travel. Was I in a time travel, whatever I was in I wanted it to stop.

It was 5:00 and I was still awake, so I started making breakfast or at least try, I'm not a good cook but as I was getting things out it seemed as if I knew what I was doing. I made homemade biscuits, gravy, bacon, scrambled eggs and was cutting up some fruit when Laura walked in.

"What is going on?" she said.

"Breakfast, I made breakfast."

"John, it looks wonderful, you really surprised me."

"Go get the girls up and I am going to take a shower, but go ahead and start eating, I have to leave at 6:45."

After I was dressed I came to the kitchen, where they were eating.

"Wow, Daddy, this is great. Sorry, Mom, but Daddy, this is the best gravy I have ever eaten," said Zoe.

Laura said she wanted to take lessons and the girls started laughing.

Madison said, "Aren't you going to eat?"

I told her I already ate but I hadn't because Jayden didn't want me to eat after midnight. I said, "I had an early appointment and will see you girls after school."

Laura walked me to the front door and gave me a kiss and hug and said she would be at the hospital after she dropped the girls off at school. "Don't worry," she said, "everything will be alright."

When I walked into the hospital, Jayden was in the hall and told me to come with him. He had the lab ready for me and as soon as they were finished drawing blood they were going to take me to a room and the x-ray tech would come and get me, when Laura got there they would bring her to my room and wait. Then after they were ready for me to view the scan they would call me and I would get over here soon as I got a break.

"Listen, John," he said, "we are good friends and whatever is going on we will fix it." He shook my hand and told me to relax.

It was about 20 minutes later, then the x-ray tech came and got me. They gave me a gown and told me to put it on, then come into room 3. As I walked into the room, the tech told me to lay down on the table and put the earphones on. As I lay there I heard a voice asking what kind of music did I want to listen to.

"Classic rock from the 70s."

"Classic rock it is."

The voice came on saying for me to stay very still and just relax, this would take about 45 minutes, then the music came on. I lay there in the dark, listening to music, I must have dozed off.

As the alarm clock went off, Shelby said, "Get up, it's morning." She rolled over and gave me a hug. "I have to leave and go to the house and get ready. Get up and take a shower, then I will be by to pick you up at 7:45." She got up and left.

I lay there almost in tears, why did I come back here? Maybe the test here and the test in my real life had something in common, maybe this was the end of this nightmare. I took a shower, then went into the kitchen and went outside to feed Sam. I just sat at the table when Shelby came through the front door.

"Let's go, babe," she said, "I know I am 5 minutes late."

As Shelby was driving I thought about calling Taylor and telling him we were going to be a few minutes late, but I forgot there were no cell phones in 1975, how times have changed.

Once at the hospital we walked in to the desk and told them who I was, then a doctor came up to me and said he was Dr. Ron Henry, friend of Dr. Taylor, and he was going to run some tests.

"Dr. Taylor told me of your dreams and all that was happening now and the future. We have just installed a new x-ray machine, it's called a CAT scan machine. It shows different levels of your brain in a whole new way. We are going to look into your brain and see if there is something abnormal in there."

"Dr. Henry—"

"Please call me Ron," he said.

"Okay, Ron, how long before you get the results?"

"Well," he said, "it should take about 3-4 hours after we are finished with the scan. Dr. Taylor wanted me to call him when I was ready to view the pictures and we could talk together as I was seeing what I found. He wanted me to send a copy of the scan with you and take it over to him at Blue Rock Memorial and he would go over them with you. Any questions?" he asked.

"None that I can think of," I said.

"Shelby, you can wait in the waiting room, and Greg, come with me."

After I was in the room they told me to take my shirt off and get onto the table. A nurse put an earphone around my head, it was a circle and uncomfortable, she said to lay still and not move or they would have to do another one. As I lay on the table I was moved into this huge round tube and it was noisy and seemed liked it took forever, then finally I was moved out of the tube and the nurse came and removed the donut-looking thing off from around my head. She took me to the room Shelby was in and said the doctor would be right in.

When Ron came in he told me to take this package to Dr. Taylor and he would go everything with me. We left the hospital and headed to Blue Rock.

We didn't say a word in the car, and we arrived at the hospital. We got out and Shelby held my hand as we walked to the front door. We went to the desk and asked if they could tell Dr. Taylor we were here. After about 30 minutes they called us back and took us to his office, where he was sitting.

"Here are the pictures," Shelby said.

"Well," as he took them out and was looking, he said that Dr. Henry said he couldn't find any mass or anything that would cause my brain to have abnormal reactions to sleep. So the next step was a sleep study, they would hook a machine up to my brain and would put me into a deep sleep, then study my brainwaves. I called my friend Joseph, who does sleep study and was very interested in doing a study. In fact, he was doing a counseling class on sleep study and wanted to do it this afternoon after his class.

"Is that alright with you, Greg?"

"Sure," I said, "what time?"

He said his class was over at 2:00 and he was about 90 minutes away, "so let's say be here at 3:30 because I have to bring my machine with me and unload it and get it ready. Why don't you two go have a nice lunch, then be back here at 3:30?"

"Sounds good," Shelby said, "I am hungry."

We went to a restaurant that was famous for ribs, we walked in and sat at a table. A waitress came and brought us a menu, she said, "Hello, Greg," I said hello back. She said her dog, Black Jack, was a different dog after she picked him up from me. Never thought anyone could have trained him the way I did, she was very pleased.

"Good to hear," I said.

Shelby said she wanted ribs and fries with coleslaw and tea.

"Make that two orders," I said.

As we sat there I told Shelby that whatever happened, that if I went to sleep and didn't come back to this time zone or wake up not remembering the last few days not to be mad or hurt. "Maybe the other Greg will come back, whatever or whoever is with you just remember they are lucky to be with you."

Just then a huge plate of ribs was placed in front of me, piled high with fries.

"Enjoy," said the waitress.

We ate, they were very good ribs, I wasn't much on the sauce but the ribs were tender and smokey.

After we ate I asked Shelby if she wanted to take a walk around the town, we had time to spare. She said that would be great. So we drove to town and parked the car and got out and started walking, people waved and said hi, I just waved back, pretending I knew who they were. Shelby said she needed some nail polish, so we stopped in this little store and she bought 4 bottles of polish. We walked down the street and at the end was a park, so we went and sat on the bench under this oak tree. Shelby said she wanted a malt from the drug store and asked if I wanted one.

"No way, not after those ribs, but go ahead, I will hold your bag."

As she went across the street to the drugstore I sat there. I was looking up at the tree and was looking at names people wrote on the limbs. I looked inside the bag and took out a bottle of polish, it was orange-red color. I went to this huge limb and with the nail polish I wrote "John 2020-1975." Then when it dried I put a coat of clear polish on top of it. I sat back down just as Shelby walked over to me, and I said, "We better get going so we won't be late."

We parked the car at the hospital and Shelby took out a Polaroid camera and took 2 pictures of us, she gave me one and she kept the other.

"This way you can never forget me."

It felt weird holding hands as we walked into the hospital but I felt sad for her, she was so sweet.

Taylor saw us and told us to come with him. "Joseph just got here so it will be a few minutes." He told Shelby she might as well go home, that I was going to be here all night and she could come by in the morning, around 9:00, to see what we decided.

Shelby gave me a hug and kissed me, saying, "Sweet dreams."

Joseph came into the room and explained what all he was going to do. "Now take off your shirt and lay on the bed as I hook you up."

Taylor said he had to leave but I was in good hands, he would check on me later.

Joseph gave me this sour drink and told me to drink all of it. After the challenge of drinking that glass of sour lemonade taste, he told me to just relax and lay still. He turned out the light and turned on the machine and he left the room.

I heard a voice coming through the headphones saying the scan was completed and that I did good at keeping still. They took me in the bed I was into a room where I heard, "There's Daddy, he is back! He is awake!"

The girls squeezed my hand and Laura leaned over the bed and kissed me with tears running down her cheeks.

"What is wrong?" I asked.

Jayden was there beside my bed. "John, what is the last thing you remember?"

I said, "I was in a sleep study in 1975."

No one said a word.

He asked, "Do you remember anything about your accident?"

"I had a dream I was in one but it was only a dream. Did that really happen?"

"Yes, you broke your left arm and for the last 3 days you were in a coma. You had a small bleed in your head, but we just did another scan and there is no more bleeding. You just woke so this is the first time your family has seen you awake. Just rest."

"Wait," I said, "what about my dreams?"

He told me my body had been through a lot, I should just rest, we will talk later.

"Are you alright, was anyone in the car with me?"

"No, just you, someone ran a stop sign. You don't remember that?"

"No," I said.

"Get some rest, we can talk later."

"No," I said, "tell me now."

Laura told me everything about the morning of the accident. "The hospital called me at the shop and told me you were in the emergency room. They couldn't wake you up, your head was bleeding, arm was broken but not waking up was the big issue. Finally after 3 days, 3 horrifying days and nights, you woke up."

I looked at them and said, "I am so sorry for scaring you, it must have been awful."

Jayden came back in with some film, saying, "Everything looks good." He told Laura to take the kids down to the cafeteria, he wanted to look at me more closely.

"Well, John, I am pleased with the test, maybe in a couple of days you can go home. Laura has been here day and night, I am going to tell Laura that I am calling Trinity to go stay at your house tonight so Laura can get some sleep, she needs it."

"Thanks, Taylor."

"Well, I am going to tell Laura the plans," he said, "while you get some rest."

A knock at the door and this nurse came in with a tray of food. "Good morning, breakfast time."

I just lay there for a moment, then realized I was still here.

"How did you sleep?" she asked.

"I guess alright, don't remember any after Taylor left."

"Here is your breakfast, enjoy."

After I finished all my breakfast Laura and the girls came in. Laura said the girls wanted to see me before school.

I said, "Glad you did."

"Daddy, can we autograph your cast?"

"Yes, you may," I said.

They signed their names and drew a happy face on it.

"We need to go, girls, school is about to start."

After a kiss they walked out and I asked Laura how she slept.

"Like a log, Trinity came over so I went to sleep at 8:00 and didn't wake up until this morning."

"Get going," I said, "and I will see you this afternoon."

"Can't wait," she said as she walked out.

Taylor came in to check on me and said I was doing great. "I think one more night, then home you will go. Keep up the good work," he said.

The nurse came and picked up my tray and gave me some pills to take. I felt really good, I lay there and turned the TV on, it was the news, a local news channel. During the news they always show news around the nation. Then on the national news was headlines about a town in Texas called Blue Rock. The city wanted to make a park into a parking lot for a upcoming strip mall. But the citizens were all gathered around this big oak tree. The tree was over 300 years old, citizens were tearing signs saying "Save our tree," as the camera was filming the protest they zoomed in on the tree. There was a squirrel climbing a limb. The cameraman zoomed in on the squirrel and there it was: "John 2020-1975."